by Conrad Richter

These are BORZOI BOOKS, *published in New York*
by ALFRED A. KNOPF

THE ARISTOCRAT

THE

ARISTOCRAT

Conrad Richter

New York

ALFRED·A·KNOPF

1968

THE CENTRAL CHARACTER in this novel together with her parents and a few of the relatives are based in part on actual people. The other characters do not represent and are not intended to represent any real persons but are, along with the story incidents of the novel, purely imaginary and fictitious.

THIS IS A BORZOI BOOK

PUBLISHED BY ALFRED A. KNOPF, INC.

For Mary and Stuart

THE ARISTOCRAT

Chapter i

T TROUBLED me when my father told me that from
now on Miss Alexandria wanted me to sleep in her house.

"But why?" I protested.

"She says she wants a man in the house at night," my
father said dryly.

"Then why don't you sleep over?"

"She doesn't want me," my father said, and I saw by
the shape of his mouth that this was as far as I had better
go.

In those days I had no talent for philosophy, no under-
standing of the reluctance of man or boy to accept the
changes that fate proposes, changes which in later years
he may not have missed for the world. I have since specu-
lated this might also apply to man's general reluctance
toward the change called death. But then I was only fifteen years old and considered death the monstrous unknown to be avoided at all costs, mentally as well as
physically, not only for myself but for my father and for

Miss Alexandria who, so long as she lived, was the source of our security, welfare and standing in the community.

Somewhere Stevenson speaks of the ugly images he endured of his father's decline, sickness and approaching death. No doubt images of my own concerning what would happen to Miss Alexandria were at the root of my aversion, for in her early eighties she seemed ancient as the Sphinx to me. It was one of the laws of nature, I knew, that she come to her eventual demise but I did not feel it required of me to sleep in an adjoining room where I would be constantly present and aware of her slow and frightening dissolution.

There were other contributions to the gloomy prospect of living in the big house: its dark recesses that I would now have to inhabit at midnight, the musty atmosphere I must breathe along with the visible and invisible influences of the long past which I fancied at times I could actually smell, and the fact that I was to become a member of Miss Alexandria's household on this day of all days when work had been started on the building next door which she had so bitterly and vainly opposed. Yesterday or tomorrow would have been bad enough. Today was intolerable.

But when evening came, there was no help for it. There I was with my pajamas and scanty blue bathrobe in my arms escorted by my father up the street like Isaac, I thought, taken by his father Abraham into the mountain to be slain at God's bequest.

The Aristocrat

Miss Alexandria's great house, set in dark Norway spruces back from the street, stood on the same street as our own. My father was its major-domo. At least that's what Miss Alexandria sometimes called him. He ran the furnace, took care of the yard, refreshed Miss Alexandria with the town news and was general handy man around the place. Not that this was his only job. He tended bar at times at the Fire House and was deputy sheriff of the county, a post that Miss Alexandria with her influence in the party had got for him. But he would drop everything at a call from her for which he received no wages, only such gifts as the privilege of living in her grandfather's colonial house rent and tax free together with a veiled promise that the house was to be his at her death along with other considerations.

"The Morleys could never get along without your father," Miss Alexandria was fond of saying to me, "and your father could never get along without the Morleys. Everything he is he owes to this house."

From childhood that house had been nearly as familiar to me as our own. Almost daily I was sent into it to carry some message to Miss Alexandria or my father. I felt a certain pride to push in the impressive front door without knocking, especially in front of passersby, as if I were a Morley myself which one eighth of me happened to be. But once inside, the impressive high-ceilinged rooms cut me down to size as did the ancient silence. Most of the Morleys were stone-deaf in their later years. Miss Alexandria used to say that she could kill with good grace two of her ancestors, one who had introduced deafness in the Morley blood, the other, asthma in the Fortunes, and if she had a broom handle long enough she would give a good rap to the star under which she had inherited both. At the same time and almost in the same breath she would declare that deafness was a blessing. It freed her from the ravings of bores and madmen, and in the end would save her from hearing the world blow up as it gave every indication it would soon do. For a time she had a flashing light attached to her doorbell so she could answer it herself when Fanny, her one remaining maid, was away, but it could be seen only in the library and she let it get permanently out of order, instructing callers, against the advice of my father, to enter freely when there was no answer to their ring and hunt her up in the house wherever she might be.

I had always done just that, first downstairs and then up. Sometimes I found her resting from a spell of asthma in her bedroom. The door stood constantly open. I would advance gingerly and touch her on the shoulder, whereupon she would sit up and ask me to turn my face toward the light so she could read my lips. Fanny, who slept at home since her husband's recent illness, seldom arrived before eight in the morning and more than once I have seen George Moody, the painter, or Frank Goebel, the contractor, both of whom had worked on the house since boys, arrive at seven to do some work and trudge upstairs to find her.

"I'm here, Miss Alexandria," one or the other would say, touching her on the shoulder. "Now tell me what you want done," and Miss Alexandria would sit up in bed, lifting the sheets with her to cover her shrunken breasts and not the slightest embarrassment to be instructing them in the privacy of her bedroom.

Her unruffled composure was with her as usual tonight as she greeted my father and me. The thin regal nose that could lift so high bent toward me as a gracious friend while she thanked me for consenting to come as if I were conferring a favor and had volunteered of my own free will. It was uncanny to me how effortlessly she could carry on a conversation, and tonight she gave not the slightest acknowledgment of the trouble next door, speaking only good-humored phrases, poking a little fun at herself for living here alone and defenseless, hoping that I would be comfortable in her house and assuring me that my presence would mean a great deal to her peace of mind.

Frail but indomitable she ran determinedly up the thickly carpeted front stairs to show us to my room.

"I'm only sorry Fanny won't be here before school time to get your breakfast, Tommy," she said. "But your father knows my stomach rebels if I try to put anything into it before ten or eleven in the morning, and then it dare be no more than a cup of tea and a little Melba toast."

"That's all right, Miss Alexandria," my father said. "He'll have his breakfast at our house."

"Thank you, Martin. He will have his other out-of-school meals with me," she declared. "Just the same, I don't like his leaving my house in the morning on an empty stomach. It's contrary to the way we Morleys were brought up. I'd come down and get his breakfast myself but I know you'd never allow that?" She gazed keenly at my father who shook his head and smiled as if a Morley getting breakfast for a Gault was a good joke. His rugged face was always at its best when he spoke to her. An expression of mingled respect and admiration softened it such as I had seldom seen since my mother, who had a quarter of Morley blood, had passed on when I was seven. In later years I often wished I had a photograph of my father snapped while greeting or listening to Miss Alexandria.

That first night I lay awake a long time unable to sleep in the unfamiliar bed, uneasily aware of all the Morley belongings here and downstairs, the frowning portrait of a foreign priest in red robes, the great canvas of a black dog in his kennel ready to spring on chickens outside, the lifelike statue of an olive-colored Moor with his zither which would give out eery sounds when you plucked it, and the two ceremonious Savonarola chairs. I could also feel something overwhelming from the massive framed photograph of Hadrian's Tomb hanging over one of the red leather chairs in the library and the red leather couch where, my father said, Captain Morley used to take his nap of an afternoon with nothing over him but a pillow on his stomach to help his digestion.

Visitors claimed that the house had more antiques than a museum but Miss Alexandria never used the word. A furnishing was simply what it was, a Delacroix water color from Paris or the Bokhara rug that Blanche had picked up in Asia, Aunt Sudy's bureau from Maryland or the table that Grandfather Morley used to play dominoes on. All exhaled the unmistakable Morley smell which greeted me whenever I stepped into the house so that sightless I would have known where I was. The smell was particularly prevalent in the Captain's bedroom which no one used any more. Miss Alexandria called it the President's room, saying her father had had the bed made for Mr. Lincoln when he came to Gettysburg to make his celebrated speech but that he had to go back to Washington without sleeping in it. I was never sure how much was fact or fancy since she also called it the Mormon bed, pointing out that it was long and wide enough for Brigham Young and his seven wives.

"And there poor Father had to lie alone with only one wife to his name and she in the next room," she told upstairs callers. "But then Mother was hard to live with as seven. Not only for us children but for Father. She never let him get into her bed even for a nap, claiming he smelled too much of tobacco, and how they had seven children, I don't know."

Those seven children rose up in the night to trouble me, not so much the three who had lived as the four who had died, all with black diphtheria within a few days of each other. Fanny told me that old Mary, one of the maids, claimed she had seen them more than once at midnight marching out of the rooms they died in, down the front stairs, and out the double front doors on their way to the cemetery.

Whenever I awoke that night I could see them in my mind along with the three who had lived, including Miss Blanche who had married and Miss Hope who had not. Both were gone now but stories of them still lingered in the town. It was said that the Morley girls were "women of the world," that they had been the first of their sex to smoke cigarettes in the county, that the boys of town used to peep through the windows to watch them, that Miss Alexandria had set up a furore by smoking in the dining room of the Anthracarbona Hotel in Chamber City, that she had been in love with a first cousin from Maryland and wanted to marry him but her parents had bundled her off to stay with her sister, Hope, abroad until she was over it, and it was a wonder she ever came home as she was, for Miss Hope, people said, had had a baby at sixteen in the Morley attic, the baby whisked away at night to Philadelphia and Miss Hope hustled off to Europe where she became a concert pianist, the pupil of Moszkowski, and had a salon frequented by distinguished people. Some claimed that the Hope Somebody who came regularly over the years to visit the Morleys was exactly the same age as Miss Hope's child would have been. She had since died abroad along with her husband who was in the army and her daughter Hope was the one who visited Miss Alexandria now.

When I asked my father, he emphatically denied the stories, but then he would admit nothing unflattering to the Morleys. All he would say was that he had once seen Miss Hope, himself, when she came back to America on a visit, that she was a striking woman with a streak of white in the middle of her black hair, that she could speak seven languages and he had sat out in the darkness on the side porch and heard her play the piano as well as Paderewski.

Sometime during the night I got up and looked out of the window. It was moonlight and beyond the shadows of the great Norway spruces the first lines of the invading apartment house next door were clearly visible, the dark excavation of the cellar, the huge caterpillar digger with its long neck and shovel like a modern dinosaur standing over it, and to one side a mammoth truck to haul the clay away, all shimmering in the unreal light like the trappings of some Martian civilization. It gave me the

strange feeling that I lived in one era and Miss Alexandria
in another, and that what was happening next door was
only the first of a series of disasters contrived for her by
Time which I would be forced to witness and be troubled
over.

Chapter ii

THE FOLLOWING week Miss Alexandria had one of her worst asthma attacks. Not that she said anything to me but I was aware that she spent most of her time in her room. I would see her as I passed, either sitting rigid and exasperated on a chair or little more than a motionless ripple under the counterpane in her bed. She came down for supper and the evening but spoke little at the table.

"You must excuse me, Tommy," she said. "I am not fit company for children."

What bothered my father was that she had had no doctor and would have none since her good friend, Dr. Ned Temple, had died. One afternoon after school I didn't know whether to be relieved or concerned when I heard her ask Fanny to get the new doctor on the telephone. Both of them went to the open closet under the front stairs.

"Is this Dr. Howell?" I heard Fanny ask respectfully.

"Miss Alexandria wants to talk to you." There was shuffling for a moment as the two women exchanged instrument and cord, then Miss Alexandria spoke in the unmistakable, cracked voice of the long deaf, a very positive, arid voice used to being obeyed. "Dr. Howell? This is Alexandria Morley. I'd like you to come and see me. Do you know where I live? Now I can't hear what you say. If you don't know, anybody can tell you. If you ring and there's no answer, it means neither Fanny nor Tommy are here. You better not ring but walk right in and hunt me up. Most people do. If I'm not downstairs, I'll be up. I shall look for you. Good-bye." Click, and I knew she had hung up.

I went up to my room wondering how the new doctor would fare with her, having seen him about town, a tall lanky young man with tow hair and short speech. As a rule, Unionville people came promptly at Miss Alexandria's call but I listened in vain now for the sound of the front door. She and I were at supper when the bell rang and Fanny had to come from the kitchen to answer it. A moment or two later the yellow-haired doctor with bag in hand came pushing into the dining room.

"Good evening," Miss Alexandria greeted him calmly although it was only a little after five o'clock. I knew her coolness derived from his delay. "You must be Ned's young man. Won't you come over and sit down and have some supper so I can have a good look at you?"

He stared.

"I don't have time," he told her. "I'll be eating later after my evening office hours."

"I can't hear a word you say," she informed him serenely. "If you don't come by me and sit down and put your face toward the window, I can't read your lips and you might as well be speaking Hindustani."

At that he moved toward the window but he didn't sit down.

"Now if you'll tell me your trouble?"

"You must enunciate clearly if you want me to understand what you are saying," she told him but evidently she had gathered what he said for she went on, "When you learn to know us better, Dr. Howell, you'll find that we are not as others here. Mother was from Maryland. Your predecessor, Dr. Ned, used to say, when he came in this house he shut the door on Unionville. He spent practically every evening of his life in this house, drinking ale and highballs and playing cards. He was from Maryland, too. I hoped you would be the same."

"I'm from New Jersey," the doctor said shortly.

"Well," she answered as if to make the best of it. "I always said that nothing good could come out of Hoboken but I could be mistaken. Ned gave you a great send-off before he died. He saw you in medical school or someplace. He told us, that's the young man I want to see coming to your house."

The doctor looked incredulous. He shifted his bag.

"You called me?" he reminded.

"I asked you to come," she agreed with almost danger-ous sweetness. "I heard you were in town and wanted to see what sort of young man Ned had picked out for us. Oh, I expect you to charge me for the call. Like my father I pay my bills regularly twice a year, the butcher and grocer, Ida May for the daily paper and Dora at the Miners' House where I eat sometimes when Fanny is ill, and the dear little turkey man who has been bringing our chickens for half a century or thirty years at least. The only person I ever had trouble with was your friend, Ned. He never gave us a bill in his life. He said he owed us for the pleasant hours he spent in this house, not counting all the Scotch and Irish whisky he drank. Of course, Father insisted on giving him a yearly present for preserving our lives. He did just that. Now I hope you'll be agreeable and give me a bill for your calls."

"I send statements to everybody who doesn't pay cash," the doctor said. "But not for social calls. If there's nothing I can do for you—"

"You can take away this old hay fever," she told him. "Oh, I don't mean cure it. I know nobody can do that. But you can take it out and throw it in the canal. Or better yet, give it to the rude man from the Hegins Valley who's building this monstrosity of an apartment house next door so I can't sit at my bedroom window any more. My mother sat in that bay window for fifty years. She could see up the street to Uncle Asa's house. Every morn-ing he would come out and wave to her and she'd wave back at him. He wanted to marry her before Father did but she said no. She could say, no, very well. She could do anything with Uncle Asa. She told him to take Father in as a partner in the mines and he did."

The doctor didn't seem to hear. He was opening his bag and taking out stethoscope and sphygmomanometer. I watched him as he examined her. Dr. Ned had always cautioned my father to watch Miss Alexandria, that she had advanced cardiac asthma and might need help at any moment. Now I saw something come into the young doctor's eyes.

"You feel all right?" he questioned when he was through.

"I've never felt all right in my life," she informed him. "An eminent surgeon in Philadelphia told me I didn't have a normal organ in my body."

The doctor stood looking at her with narrowed eyes.

"You ever been to a specialist for what you call your hay fever?"

"A specialist?" she repeated with scorn. "I know all about specialists. You put yourself in his hands and spend five thousand dollars until you get through. You daren't wear furs or look at a dog or cat or have a flower in the house or sleep on a down pillow but on some hard lumpy mattress and wear a night dress that makes you look like the devil."

The doctor started putting some pills in a small envelope. She looked at them and pushed them back.

"Don't you have any of those nice green ones?" she asked.

"We don't prescribe according to color, Miss Morley," he said coolly.

"Well, that's the only kind does me any good. When Ned was still alive I used to go to his office and pick out my own medicine. He would howl and scream, but I asked him who had a better right since I knew more about myself than anybody else? One time when I was at Fay's I went in the office from the living room and helped myself. Next time I told him I wanted some more of those nice red pills. 'Which red ones?' he asked me. 'Show me one.' 'I can't,' I said. 'I took them all.' He had me point them out next time I came to the office. 'Good Lord, you didn't take those!' he said. 'They're just for men.' "

The young doctor looked grim.

"I can't let any patient prescribe for herself," he said.

"Oh, I have no intention of coming to your office as I did Ned's. I dislike waiting rooms and having women tell me about their hemorrhoids."

He scowled and soon departed but not before saying he would check her in about a week.

"If you need me, you know where to call," he said shortly and left.

Miss Alexandria was silent for a time after he had gone.

"Tommy," she told me at length, as if discussing some world problem, "Mother always said that medical and divinity schools should have courses in good manners. Dr.

Ned didn't need it, but then he came from Maryland. Not sixty miles from where Mother was born. All my life I've had to train girls in this house and kitchen. I thought my training days were over. Now I see I still have work to do."

Chapter iii

FROM THAT day on Miss Alexandria was definitely better. A light sparked her gray eyes. It couldn't have been the medicine, for I noticed she took hardly any of what Fanny religiously laid out for her. Then on Saturday after giving her the mail, I found her suddenly ill. She had me run upstairs for her atomizer. She went to bed soon after. Sunday morning she came down after her customary breakfast in bed. At eleven thirty she told Fanny to call Dr. Howell.

About twelve thirty the doorbell rang. The doctor came in and started to run up the stairs, evidently expecting to find his patient in bed. I told him Miss Alexandria was in the library where he found her regally dressed as if expecting a guest, which she was although he didn't know it then.

"Dr. Howell, I've had hellish news," she greeted him. "It's brought on the diabolical indigestion of the Fortunes. My mother had it. My Cousin Richard had it. My dear

Aunt Sudy had it. Our Grandmother Fortune would get it so bad she'd stand at the newel post after dinner bent over like a fishhook. She'd swear she was dying. Grandfather and I and my sister Blanche and Aunt Sudy who was my real aunt and Aunt Phi who was my colored aunt would have to work over her and get her corsets off and manipulate the gas out of her till she revived. I'm just as bad only I have no Grandfather or Blanche or Aunt Sudy or Aunt Phi to come to my rescue."

The doctor heard her impassively.

"I'll leave you something after I check you." He had already opened his bag.

At that moment Fanny in a maid's light-blue dress with freshly starched white apron, cuffs and headdress, appeared in the doorway.

"Dinner is served, Miss Alexandria," she announced and withdrew.

"Oh, damn!" Miss Alexandria said. "Now the food will get cold and that will be deadly. Doctor, you must stay to dinner and go over me afterward. As a favor to a lady's digestion," she added and without waiting for an answer, "Fanny, set a place for Dr. Howell."

"Yes, ma'am." This from Fanny who had waited knowingly just inside of the dining room.

"I shouldn't let you eat at the Miners' House at any time," Miss Alexandria went on in her positive way that admitted no disputing. "Not that Dora can't cook. She was trained right here in my own kitchen. Her trouble is she doesn't have to for Unionville. It's different when she knows I'm coming. Then she gets out her butter and sauces. She knows I'll call her for it if she doesn't. I never eat there unless Fanny's husband has one of his bad spells at home and then I manage with my own teacup and saucer that Dora keeps on her shelves for me, and my own silver that I take along."

I watched the doctor's face. From where he stood he could look out into the dining room at the inviting spectacle of snowy cloth and napkins, sterling silver and English china, a far cry from the Miners' House with its imitation marble-top tables, paper napkins and sauce and ketchup bottles, not to mention the jukebox in the corner. Here I'm sure he could also smell, as I could, the fragrance of Fanny's roasting chicken and baking pies.

"You can wash your hands in Blanche's bathroom at the head of the stairs," Miss Alexandria told him.

"I don't need to go to the bathroom," he answered brutally. He seemed vexed with her for trying to manage his life and at himself for being tempted.

Once seated in the dining room he ate ravenously enough. Single-handed Miss Alexandria kept the conversation, if such it was, going. During dessert she broke the "hellish" news that had made her ill. Her cousin Eulalie was coming to visit her. I had often seen the old lady. Her married name was Mrs. Ferguson but she was known to Fanny and my father in the Southern fashion as Miss Eulalie.

"I wouldn't call that bad," the doctor told her, un-impressed. "It should do you good, take your mind off your asthma."

"I'm sure you know medicine and stand very high in your profession," Miss Alexandria said distinctly. "But you don't know Eulalie. Most people today have the common decency to go to a hotel or what they call a motel. Eulalie is Victorian and the Victorians descended on you and stayed. 'Come and spend a month with us,' Mother used to say. She could. She kept in her room right over our heads and came down only on special occasions. Blanche and I had to do everything, look after her guests, entertain them, see there was enough food in the kitchen and that the maids went through their paces. All year long our house swarmed with company. At least once a week Aunt Caroline would come across the street in her wrapper just at dinner time. 'I baked a loaf of bread for you, Lolly,' she'd say, and Mother would tell Alice or Fanny or Polly or whoever was here to take it and set another place at the table. And there that old woman would sit and tell our guests all her troubles. At the end of the meal Mother would say, 'We just baked a cake, Caroline.' She always said 'we' though she never went near the kitchen. 'I'll have half of it cut for you to take home.' Oh, I could have killed both of them with good grace. And after a month of Eulalie, I want to poison her, too."

The young doctor didn't even smile.

"I can give you something for your nerves but you'll have to use your own strychnine."

I saw Miss Alexandria's eyes dance at him. That was the kind of talk she relished.

"I knew there was hope for you, Doctor," she said. "That you'd understand."

"I don't," he said. "If you don't want her, why do you invite her?"

"Yes, why do I? I guess because she's my cousin and I always did and Eulalie expects it and writes how hot it gets in Sweetwater in the summertime and how homesick she is to see me and the old house, and I take the easiest way out and then kick myself for a month."

"Well, I'll leave something for you," he told her. "Take it regularly and you should get through. She can't be as bad as you say."

All week I wondered if the doctor hadn't spoken too soon. As he pushed briskly up the brick walk to the house Sunday, I saw my father step out of the shrubbery to intercept him. I knew he was asking for medicine for his rheumatism as he always had Dr. Temple. The young doctor listened silently, gave my father a packet or two of pills after which he headed for the house. But his relief was short-lived. Just inside the front door I saw him stop in his tracks at the sight of a little old woman in black rising from one of the red leather chairs in the library, her eyes kindling on him from behind her glasses.

"You must be Alix's Dr. Howell?" she said busily. "I recognize you by your medicine bag. Alix has told me all about you and how much she thinks of you and how like Dr. Temple you are, or Ned, as Alix always called him. I suppose she told you that I'm Mrs. Ferguson, her cousin from Maryland. We've not only been like sisters but dear friends all our lives. But then we should, since my father and her mother were brother and sister. Alexandria was the fortunate one. She inherited a great deal of money. What little I have comes from my poor husband. Captain Ferguson was in the Navy and every Navy yard we went to, the doctors did what they could for me but they could never make me well. Once they thought it was diabetes and then a cyst and another time something else I won't pronounce. Dr. Temple thought for a while I had a hiatus hernia. Won't you sit down, Doctor, and I'll tell you all about it."

Aversely he took one of the red leather chairs, pushing his medicine bag as far out of sight as possible. It must have been plain to him by this time that like my father she had been laying for him. Now she talked on in what would have been an unending stream if Miss Alexandria hadn't appeared suddenly in the doorway, when the monologue faltered and stopped.

"Your nice young doctor has been talking to me, Alix," she said. "He's all that you said and more. I'm sure he'll be able to do something for me while I'm here."

I saw a look pass between Miss Alexandria and the doctor.

"Will you excuse Dr. Howell, Eulalie, while he helps me with the cocktails?" she said and I saw the doctor spring eagerly to his feet. Miss Alexandria paused with an ironic face in the doorway. "I suppose you want your root beer, Eulalie?" she asked with disgust.

"No, not root beer before dinner, Alix. Just a bit of tomato juice if Fanny can find any for me, or orange juice. Just so it isn't alcohol. Down in Sweetwater I get the best tomato juice, just thirty-nine cents for a huge can that lasts me several weeks. When I was young nobody touched tomatoes, let alone tomato juice."

"Your father wasn't averse to alcohol." Miss Alexandria gave a parting shot.

"No, they didn't know about tomato juice when he was a boy, not even about tomatoes. They thought they were poison. Now we know they're filled with vitamins and that alcohol is a poison. Isn't it funny to look back on those dear old people and the funny ideas they had? They thought alcohol wouldn't hurt them."

The dinner that followed was a treat to me if not to the doctor. Miss Alexandria had warned me about Miss Eulalie, instructing me how to deal with her, not to let her talk too long or I wouldn't get my homework done, never to question her about anything, under no circumstances about the Navy, but to stay out of her reach as my father had learned to do.

"Your father knows Miss Eulalie," Miss Alexandria went on. "You think you do, too, but you don't. Talking is a chronic disease with her. It's your duty to take prophylactic steps to control it. When she runs on too long with you, don't hesitate to interrupt her. Get her into an argument, anything to throw a sprag, as Uncle Asa used to say, into her wheel. If that fails, you must take it on yourself to politely insult her. Oh, I know it's blasphemy. Children should be seen and not heard. But you must learn to protect yourself. She's very sweet and won't take offense. If she does look hurt for a while, you must harden your heart. Remember you're applying therapy."

I nodded but knew I wouldn't have the courage. Just the same, I felt complimented and all through dinner watched Miss Alexandria's performance, a word she was very fond of using. She would stop her cousin with a whole battery of interruptions.

"I can't hear a thing you say, Eulalie," she would break in. "You don't move your lips when you talk."

"I was never taught to," Miss Eulalie protested. "So many people show all their teeth in their photographs. I was brought up to keep my mouth closed."

Miss Alexandria gave the doctor a despairing look and let her cousin run along for a while about Sweetwater and the Fortune plantation of a thousand acres along the Potomac where she and Miss Alexandria had run wild as children, always under the protection of a colored eye.

"We're so devoted, Alix and I," Miss Eulalie went on. "We've written to each other every week for thirty-two years and I can tell you everything we ever said to each other. We write on the same day each week. I sit down in Maryland and know Alix is writing me up here in Pennsylvania. I write every Sunday evening at nine o'clock and Alix writes me every Sunday morning at eleven."

"I don't have anything to do then," Miss Alexandria said glumly. "But I can write a letter."

Miss Eulalie looked hurt. She mentioned that Miss Alexandria might go to church, then took refuge in her lot at Arlington where she would be buried beside Jack one day. From there she went on to Jack's final illness and funeral. When it grew too long, Miss Alexandria tartly interrupted again. She told the doctor about her cousin, Richard, vice president of a Chamber City bank, how he loved Unionville and made it a point to come home to it early every afternoon.

"I don't see how he could leave the bank early if he put in an honest day's work," Miss Eulalie mentioned.

"He was vice president and could do as he pleased. No one dared say anything to him. They couldn't run the bank without him. Every weekday rain or shine he left Chamber City at three thirty on the main line and there was a train waiting for him at the Junction."

"It wasn't waiting just for him," Miss Eulalie objected meekly.

"Of course, it was. If the main-line train were late, our Unionville train would wait for him."

"But not only for him. It waited for the other passengers, too."

"If there were other passengers, and there often were, they could take it, too."

"You say it as if it was Richard's train."

"Well, we always called it Richard's train. He knew the conductor and trainmen and always waved to the engineer. They knew he was coming and waited for him."

"And for everybody else on the main-line train, too."

"Well, of course. Those that wanted to could ride along. There's no law that said they couldn't. It was no private car, if that's what you mean. But it was Richard's train. Mother and Father always called it that."

Miss Alexandria gave her a triumphant look and her cousin in self-defense turned to Jack, the long hours he had given the Navy as paymaster, how he would have been an admiral had he lived, what he had told her when they first met, how handsome he looked that day in his uniform and what his fellow officers in full dress had done at the wedding. Almost immediately Miss Alexandria lost her triumph. Her lips pressed together and she grew silent. I was to learn that Jack was Miss Eulalie's trump card which she always played to put her cousin, who had never been married, in her place.

It was fascinating to me, a poor relation, but the lanky young doctor looked bored and almost mad. I could tell he was itching for Miss Alexandria to use her finger bowl, something he ignored, and to rise so he could get away. Then we heard the front door open and a fresh young voice tell my father to put her bags in Miss Blanche's room—she was never spoken of as Mrs. Rosecommon—and a girl of eighteen or nineteen rushed in and up to the table. First she kissed Miss Alexandria who rose to greet her and then Miss Eulalie who didn't.

"Hello, Fanny," she smiled to the maid and to me, ignoring the doctor.

"You haven't had your dinner!" Miss Alexandria accused.

"I couldn't when I knew yours was waiting for me. But I guess I'm too late."

"You're late, but not too late," Miss Alexandria pronounced. "I always told Blanche there were just three people I'd excuse for coming late to the table, and you're one of them. Fanny will see that you're served."

I looked at Fanny half-expecting to find her discommoded at the prospect of another mouth to feed and house guest to pick up after. Instead her face beamed and I realized that like my father she took more pleasure in the arrival of guests than her mistress.

Now Miss Alexandria remembered and introduced the doctor who with two ladies standing had continued to sit in his chair like a bump on a log, and I wondered if he knew, as I did, who Miss Hope was. It came to me that this was the perfect opening for him to pay his respects to his hostess and go. Instead he stayed glued to his chair as if unable to take his eyes off the young visitor.

"I'll run upstairs and wash my hands, Alexandria," Miss Hope said lightly. "Then I'll be right down."

Chapter iv

THE BATTLES of the two cousins fascinated me but not for long. Miss Alexandria amused but Miss Eulalie was too much the tortoise slowly winning the race. I learned to know in advance everything she would say, her thoughts and opinions, the minute incidents of her life with Jack, her every word. In time I managed the trick of shutting my ears. For her part, Miss Alexandria needed only to look away from her cousin's lips to peace and oblivion. But a Morley, she once told me, never turned tail on an adversary. Her eyes would grow pale with boredom and, at the start of some familiar repetition, glance at me with helpless anger and commiseration.

"I do give the devil his due," I heard her reply to Dr. Howell who was trying to make her see the best of it. "In thirty years I've never heard her add a word or change a line. She hasn't the imagination," she added bitterly.

My father thought the punishment she inflicted on herself by listening to Miss Eulalie frayed her nerves. He knew and feared the latter himself and stayed away from her as much as he could. If he hadn't, he told me, she would have him busy night and day with small chores and conversation.

He thought it was desperation over Miss Eulalie that brought on what happened later. I was in the upstairs hall when I heard Miss Eulalie in a flurry down at the front door.

"Oh, Doctor! Thank God you've come. I've hinted to you of the instability of the Morleys. They go off on a tangent. You know, when they can't stand anything the men go off to war. Alix bangs doors. Now the Fortunes never do that. Jack always told me a slow, creaking door hangs on its hinges the longest. Things ruffle me, of course, but I won't let my well-being be affected. But Alix is a Morley and she's started something now I'm afraid will destroy her."

He didn't ask what she was talking about, knowing better than to pry open the bung hole, but started up the stairs with Miss Eulalie in pursuit. He found Miss Alexandria on her feet in her bedroom. From the hall I heard her triumphant good morning. From my glimpse of her I thought she looked better than in a long time.

The doctor looked her over critically.

"Good morning. What do I hear you've been up to now?"

"I don't know what you mean," she said but her eyes sparkled with devilment. "Unless it's the good deed I performed yesterday." She took her skirts in hand and gave an exultant little dance which made her almost girlish for the moment. "It was something that had to be done for the morals of Anthracarbona County."

"It wasn't necessary at all, Alix," Miss Eulalie protested. "You know your Grandfather Fortune would have played dominoes."

"Yes, and that's all he ever did do. Grandmother had to go out and oversee the fieldhands. It's my responsibility, Eulalie. They went too far raising my taxes. They had to be taught a lesson."

"What's this?" the doctor asked. "My taxes haven't been raised."

"If she charged enough rent, Doctor," Miss Eulalie pleaded, "she could pay the higher taxes. You know what she rents her houses for? Six and eight dollars a month. The same as her father and grandfather Morley charged fifty years ago. And then she pays her own repairs."

"They're my people and my houses, Eulalie." Miss Alexandria spoke with dangerous calm.

"I'm not saying they're not, Alix," Miss Eulalie hurried to say. "But you can't fight the coal interests and the whole county besides. Doctor, she has only four or five houses in Primrose township. She gets thirty or forty dollars a month for all of them put together. And for that thirty or forty dollars she wants to fight the big coal companies, the county and all the rest."

"I don't know what this is all about," the doctor said.

"But I don't want you fighting anyone in your condition, Miss Morley."

"I'm not fighting anyone," she declared serenely. "They're fighting me. They own most of the township and then they don't pay their taxes. So the township people naturally have to raise taxes on everybody in the township who does pay. And that means me."

"I should think if they didn't pay, their property would be put up for taxes."

"That's how it's worked." Miss Alexandria pitied him. "They always have some political henchman buy their land back from the county. For a song. It saves them a great deal of taxes. But it robs the poor township of tax money to pay for its schools and teachers. The sheriff and judges are in on it and the people are afraid to do anything. It's why a Morley has to step in and take a hand."

"Doctor!" Miss Eulalie begged. "She's bought all the Primrose Coal and Iron land in the county. For taxes! I don't know how many thousands and thousands of acres. I said to her, 'Alix, what can you ever do with all those coal lands? You can't go out with a pick and shovel.'"

At the sound of the company name involved, the doctor looked grave. It was one of the most powerful in the county.

"Don't you think you ought to have counsel before getting into something like that?" he asked.

"I always have counsel," Miss Alexandria assured him. "I ask Fanny and Martin and sometimes Tommy and Mr.

January. Like Queen Elizabeth, I listen to all my counselors and then do as I please, and nobody can say I didn't ask other people's advice."

"What do you think you can do, Miss Morley?"

"I intend to restore moral decency in the coal business," she said. "Like in my father's generation."

"Your Uncle Asa wasn't always very moral," Miss Eulalie pointed out, carefully avoiding mention of Miss Alexandria's father who was his partner. "I understand he took money out of his miners' pay to build the Methodist church here. I believe some of the miners used to shake their fists at it when they went by."

"He did," Miss Alexandria agreed placidly. "I'm not a very religious person but I must admit that Uncle Asa performed a highly religious and moral act. Many of the miners here and in the patches were Methodists and they had no Methodist church to go to."

"Why didn't he let them build their own church if they wanted one?"

"They hadn't the will power to take the money out of their own pay envelopes. Uncle Asa had. There was nothing questionable in what he did. The United States Treasury adopted exactly the same procedure later on when they started deducting income tax from pay envelopes and for a much less worthy cause. In fact they copied Uncle Asa. He might have sued them for it if he had lived."

"Your Uncle Asa wanted the church, too," Miss Eulalie said. "I think he made himself head of the church council."

"He did," Miss Alexandria agreed. "And a very generous and philanthropic head he was, too. He let the miners pay no more than half of the church cost. The other half he paid out of his own pocket."

Dr. Howell took his instruments from the bag and proceeded to listen to his patient's heart and bronchi. He checked the blood pressure in both arms, repeating it in the right arm.

"I think you better go to bed, Miss Morley, and stay down till I see you again," he ordered grimly.

"I can't," she informed him. "I've invited the officers of the Primrose Coal and Iron Company to the house this evening."

The doctor put his instruments back into his bag.

"Have Fanny call them up and say you've changed your mind."

"I never change my mind," Miss Alexandria told him. "I'm like Mother. She changed hers only once. That was on her wedding day when she woke up with a bad headache. She told the maid she wasn't going through all that with a headache. But the more she thought about it, the more she knew it would be still more of a headache to put everything off including a hundred and fifty guests."

"You have a headache now, Alix!" Miss Eulalie said. "I can tell by the red spots in your cheeks."

"Of course I have a headache." Miss Alexander dismissed it. "I'm almost never without a headache. I'd feel there was something seriously wrong with me if I didn't have a headache. A headache keeps me on an even fighting keel so I don't do anything weak and conciliatory."

"I'm only your physician," the doctor said dryly. "But I must say you're in no condition to do any fighting."

"That's what Dr. Seyfert told my father in the sixties. Father raised a company and went through the entire campaign. His brother, Jim, too. A fight, Doctor, clears the Morley head and steadies the constitution. One time I was introduced to Christopher Morley on the platform at the Broad Street Station. When my train began to pull out, I asked him if he had the same coat of arms as we. He ran alongside on the platform. 'Bite 'em. Bite 'em!' he called after me. He knew the Morleys."

Dr. Howell remained grave. I'm not sure that he knew who Christopher Morley was.

"Well, I won't be responsible for what happens," he said flatly.

"I can tell you exactly what will happen," Miss Alexandria assured him. "I'll have a lovely time teaching these upstart coal operators a little about good manners. It's something very much lacking in this day and age."

The doctor looked skeptical as he left but I couldn't share his feeling. Miss Alexandria had already done a good deal, I noticed, to the manners of the doctor himself. He took off his hat now when he came into the hall. He stood, if sitting down, when Miss Alexandria entered the room and said good morning and good-bye civilly when he came and went. He even on occasion thanked her for his dinner and managed at times to praise some certain special dish, when she had tactfully brought him around to it.

Fanny had gone home and I answered the door that evening. Three well-dressed men stood on the porch. They asked to see Miss Morley and I took them into the library. The first glimpse I had of them on opening the door did not reassure me and after telling Miss Alexandria upstairs that she had guests, I observed them again when I said she would be down directly. Just the way they seated themselves on the red leather chairs of the library spoke power and confidence. These were no mean adversaries, I thought. It was confirmed by the respect with which Mr. January treated them when he arrived.

As I turned back from the door I saw Miss Alexandria descending the stairs, a formidable if frail figure in an elegant long green silk, her hair visibly brushed and done up, a string of small diamonds and other jewels around her neck and on her finger the huge Morley diamond ring which lighted up like a chandelier whichever way she turned it. She greeted the men in the warmly urbane way I knew so well and which she managed so perfectly with a touch of lightness as if this were no more than a friendly call.

"Alexandria likes to show off to men," Miss Eulalie had once told Hope in my hearing but Hope had said she

thought it was something else, that Miss Alexandria had
been raised with her cousin Richard, had driven her
father's and uncles' horses, had played golf, smoked cigarettes and driven a car when most women didn't do these
things. So she felt perfectly natural with men. This particular evening was warm with rain threatening and Miss
Alexandria soon took one of the men with her to the
pantry to pour highballs, after which there was a deceiv-
ingly amiable stream of voices from the library. At the
same time under the pleasant talk and tinkle of ice and
glasses, I thought I could detect along with the growing
storm a rising urgency in the visiting coal men and in Mr.
January. They seemed to be trying to get her to give up
her quixotic idea that a large corporation must pay taxes
on its vast coal lands as if it were no more than a man
with a forty-foot lot in town. Why, their colliery gave
bread and life to hundreds of local people! This was something she must try to understand. Otherwise, the whole
west end of Anthracarbona County would be hurt by
what was sure to happen.

From my book in the living room I could tell they
didn't take Miss Alexandria seriously. I don't suppose
they would have changed their minds if the storm that
had been gathering all evening hadn't suddenly descended
upon us. The artillery that for an hour or more had been
firing from the distant Second Mountain moved to the hill
called the Long Stretch overlooking the town. The in-
terval between lightning and thunder grew ominously

shorter and any man talking had to pause in the middle
of a sentence until the immediate cannonading let up.

Miss Alexandria had been reading their lips. She knew
by the interruptions and constant dimming of the lights
that something was happening. Now streaks of lightning
began invading the room through the drawn blinds.
When I crept into the hall a little fearful that the house
might be struck, I saw her gazing at the windows with a
kind of delight.

"Oh, isn't this nice!" she said, as if welcoming a friend.
She raised the blinds. "Don't you love a storm, gentlemen?"

In another moment she had turned the switch and the
library was in darkness except for the constant succession
of brilliant flashes. The whole heavens seemed inflamed.
It was one of the heaviest storms of my boyhood and fell
in full fury on us now. The sky kept splitting and the
almost instant roar showed that the bolts had not missed
Miss Alexandria's house by much.

"Isn't it magnificent!" she kept exclaiming. "I think,
gentlemen, beauty is one of our greatest natural resources
here in Anthracarbona County. It reminds me of the
storms Blanche and I used to watch breaking over the
Alban Hills in Rome."

It was a scene to remember, Miss Alexandria standing
untouched in the middle of her darkened library with the
violent green and violet lightning playing over her and
the deafening crashes about her ears while the four men

crouched on their leather chairs staring at her and at each other. Not till later did I realize that she hadn't been able to hear anything at all. By that time the storm had passed, the lights turned on and the shaken coal operators had taken their departure.

Chapter v

KNEW there was something wrong that morning
when I saw my father. Miss Alexandria had sent me over
to say she wanted to go for a ride in the afternoon. It was
a chore he had always enjoyed. When there were no
guests, Miss Alexandria would sit with him on the front
seat and relate pungent bits of history of the places they
passed. She liked especially to go up the Broad Mountain
where her father and Uncle Asa had mined, to point out
collieries past and present, tell about the people who had
owned them and of things that had happened in the mining patches.

But today my father heard her request grimly. He
asked me to tell Miss Alexandria he was sorry but he
couldn't go. He didn't feel up to it. He was sick. I looked
at him in astonishment. My father was almost never that
sick, and if he was, I felt, he would have got out of bed
to do something for Miss Alexandria. When I told her
what he had said, she ordered him to go to the doctor at

once or have Dr. Howell come to see him and I was to bring her the doctor's report.

The first light on my father's reluctance to drive out with Miss Alexandria came when Miss Eulalie sat down for dinner. She had been uptown and her eyes behind her glasses were busy with suppressed excitement.

"You always say I talk through my hat, Alix," she said while Fanny began serving. "But I told you what would happen."

Miss Alexandria took her time tasting the soup.

"Exactly what did you tell me would happen?" she asked patiently as to a child.

"I didn't say exactly. But I knew you would get into trouble buying those thousands of acres of coal lands that belong to the Primrose Colliery. Now you've shut down their colliery."

"If it's shut down, it's not because of anything I did," Miss Alexandria said tranquilly. "It's because they have too much coal on hand. This is summertime. Collieries always have too much coal on hand in the summertime and have to shut down."

"No, they say they have plenty of orders for fall. They say you shut them down because you own their land and they can't mine coal on somebody else's property. It's a pretty serious thing, Alix."

"If they have plenty of orders on hand, I can't imagine what they're shutting down for," Miss Alexandria told her. "All they need do is pay me their taxes and they can have their coal lands back. Mr. January says I couldn't keep them anyhow if it went to court."

"I don't know about that," Miss Eulalie repeated doggedly. "But I do know you've thrown all those poor miners out of work."

"I've thrown nobody out of work," Miss Alexandria declared with the calmness of Buddha or the pope. "I've simply paid the colliery's taxes so the miners' children can go back to school this fall. If the operators pay what they owe, it will be just as it was before."

"You can talk, Alix, but that doesn't give the poor men their wages. I believe three hundred lost their jobs."

"They haven't lost their jobs at all." Miss Alexandria dismissed her. "The operators aren't going to abandon their colliery because of a few taxes. They're just giving themselves and their men a holiday and taking out their spite on me. They should all be glad for a chance to help out the farmers or paint their houses. I'm surprised Primrose employs only three hundred men. When Father and Uncle Asa shut down Kalmia for the summer, there were twelve hundred men out of work, and so far as I know they all survived."

"I don't see how you can be so calloused," Miss Eulalie mumbled. "I shouldn't want three hundred starving men going around blaming me."

"They blamed Uncle Asa when he deducted contributions to build his Methodist church but the church still stands, or what's left of it. The walls didn't fall down like the walls of Jericho."

Miss Eulalie kept glumly silent. I saw that Fanny who had a son and nephew in the mines looked grave. But Miss Alexandria ate what was for her a hearty dinner with an extra helping of vanilla ice cream to go with Fanny's freshly baked apple pie.

When I spoke to my father at the end of the week, I could see he didn't like it.

"Miss Alexandria did right, understand, Tommy. She always does. She says they're her people and she has to look after them. Some did work for her father once upon a time. Just the same, I wish she hadn't done it. The miners don't see it her way. They're drinking pretty heavy these days and making threats against her. They say they'll get her. Meantime they take it out on me because I work for her. But don't breathe a word of that to her. She won't worry about herself but she will about me."

He didn't seem to care if I worried about him. I was his son and that was my business. Besides, I was young and a little worry wouldn't push me into the grave. But Miss Alexandria daren't be upset. When some unknown sniper took a shot at his deputy sheriff's car on the Broad Mountain, he squelched the report to keep it out of the *Miners' Journal*, which Miss Alexandria read every evening for news of her Chamber City friends.

Looking back, I think Miss Alexandria must have suspected something from the ticklish care with which we treated her. Perhaps, too, from the Rev. Danner's immediate and solicitous calls, as if he looked for something violent to happen to her tomorrow. He was neither Reformed or Methodist, but Lutheran, living almost next door. His merit in Miss Alexandria's eyes was as a neighbor and that he hailed from Maryland. He had made a few purely social calls in the house on that account, but now I heard his voice a great deal in the library of an evening. Some irreverent Reformed said he was trying to get money for his church in her will. He seldom rang but walked right in. He had been to Rome and the Holy Land and except for his mysterious, veiled warnings to Miss Alexandria that while we are in life we are in the midst of death, they had much to talk about together.

"The Rev. Danner doesn't believe in wines or cards but I'm doing my best to broaden him," I heard her tell Miss Eulalie. "He's such a nice young man. He always reminds me of an English vicar. I tell him he should be more worldly to cope with the sins of the world. The first time he came in this house he found me playing solitaire. He shied from the card table as if it had horns. I told him how solitaire had saved my mother's reason and more than once saved mine. After that he gave my cards a kinder look."

"You shouldn't try to corrupt a minister of the gospel, Alix," Miss Eulalie said. "God wouldn't let you anyhow."

"Nonsense," Miss Alexandria told her. "One night he

dropped in while the Schuylers were here playing bridge. I said, 'Rev. Danner, will you take my hand for a minute? I want to run upstairs for a handkerchief.' I gave him my cards and set him down in my chair. The girls said afterward he was no Ely Culbertson but he didn't do bad. Unfortunately he said he had to go as soon as I came down. But I gave him a little check as a bon voyage gift when he went to the Holy Land. He bought a rug with it over there and came back so pleased. I'm afraid the Arab rug dealer cheated him but I feel I'm making progress."

How much Miss Alexandria guessed of the reasons for the Rev. Danner's interest in her, I never knew, but I could see she was getting restless from being deprived of her rides. One day at dinner she told Miss Eulalie she didn't know what had got into my father. Here she was practically dying of an asthma attack and if Martin wouldn't take her up on the Broad Mountain, she would drive up herself.

"You wouldn't, Alix!" Miss Eulalie gave one of her aghast, sidewise looks.

"Indeed and double I would."

"You haven't driven for years."

"I haven't driven a horse either though I know I can."

"But you have no driver's license."

"Oh, that was an oversight. I went to Majorca for the winter. When I came back, my license had expired. I'd have had to take a driver's test and I wasn't up to it then."

"You aren't up to it now."

"I have a little asthma," Miss Alexandria admitted. "But as soon as I get up the mountain, it will be all right. It always is. I'll show you. I intend to take you along."

"Not me, Alix," Miss Eulalie said hastily. "I have a bad headache. I would only get worse from the bumps."

"My car doesn't bump," Miss Alexandria informed her. "But if you won't keep me company, Tommy will, won't you, Tommy?"

I felt sure my father would drive her himself sooner than let her at the wheel, but when I ran over to tell him, the house was empty. Like a sheep to the slaughter I followed her to what was once the Morley stable, bigger and finer than many Unionville houses. Now it only housed her car along with the ancient smell of horses.

Miss Eulalie had come out after us.

"You'll be arrested, Alix!" she warned.

"I'm sure all those nice young men on the state police force are trained to be polite to a lady, Eulalie. Especially a lady who drove these roads before they were born. But if I go to jail," she added serenely, "Martin will get me out."

I opened the stable doors, and got in the car reluctantly beside her. She managed to start the engine, then sat erect at the wheel, nose up, and we started for the front gate. Main Street was miraculously free of moving objects when we came out between the stone gateposts, whereupon Miss Alexandria began to sail uptown.

"I want to show the town I can still burn up the road

as I used to in Uncle Asa's car. It was the first ever owned in Anthracarbona County. I'll slow down once we get out in the country."

I glanced uneasily ahead at our only traffic light, found it red and turning green as we approached. It was a benign sign, and I felt better.

"This is North Unionville isn't it, Tommy?" she asked a minute later. "I don't remember that red barn ahead in the middle of the street."

"It's a truck, Miss Alexandria! Get over!" I begged her and she obliged in time to let a monster loaded coal truck from Virginia pass.

"The authorities should put such a driver through his paces," she told me and moved back on the median line.

Once we crossed Black Creek and headed up into the mountains, her nose which had been up like a ship's bow cleaving the air, began to lower, as she gazed around fondly on the dark, scarred mountain country. She showed me the hill where many years before a Dr. Dreher had been fatally dragged by his horse, the sad-looking house where, she said, the first man had been murdered by the Molly Maguires, and the old broken-down hotel called Paddy Moran's where the Mollies used to meet.

"Uncle Asa and Paddy got along famously," she told me. "One winter they were going down to the boiler house and Paddy fell on the ice. He had a whisky flask in his hip pocket and felt something running down his pants' leg. 'I hope to God it's blood,' he told Uncle Asa."

She stopped where her father's and Uncle Asa's colliery had once stood. The mountains of culm banks of her youth were gone, she said sadly, and there was no sign of the great black breaker, only the ruins of the stone boiler-house with the woods growing up through them. Very slowly she drove through the Primrose mining patch, pointing out the houses her father had owned before her. She spoke and smiled graciously to the idle men, women and children in the street. They stared at us. Several of the boys ran after our car when we left.

"They still know a Morley when they see one," she said with satisfaction. "They remember what we tried to do for them all our lives."

After leaving the patch, I told her that an old pick-up truck was following us. She looked pleased.

"They want to see that no harm comes to us," she nodded.

I wasn't so sure. I hadn't liked the looks the men and some of the women and children had given us. When we reached a stretch of lonely mountain road, the truck behind us started to come around. It drew up abreast but did not pass. Instead it crowded closer forcing Miss Alexandria into the ditch. Then with a ripping sound of metal and crash of glass it rammed into us, threw Miss Alexandria's car against the bank and drove on with a piece of her left fender wedged in its unpainted body frame.

Chapter vi

WHEN I picked myself up from the floor, Miss Alexandria was still in her seat holding on to the wheel. Now she started the engine which had stalled in the encounter. It ran perfectly but the car refused to budge. It made only strange jerks and grinding noises when she threw the transmission into gear. She didn't try to get out but took a cigarette from her bag. I saw now that her left arm hung limp and that blood from shattered glass was running down her face. She lighted the cigarette with her right hand and sat there erect as in the bay window at home, smoking, waiting calmly for someone to come.

Someone did come along after only a few minutes, a salesman in a light candy truck. He stopped short when he saw our car and came over.

"What happened?" he stammered.

"It was an accident," Miss Alexandria said in a tone that suggested he ask no further.

"Anybody hurt?"

"No," she told him. "We are quite all right but I'd be grateful if you would take us to my house in Unionville. My car doesn't seem to want to respond."

With a tire bar from his truck, he managed to pry open one of our doors. Then he squeezed us into the front seat of his truck. We went back through the mining patch at Primrose with the same men, women and children in the street staring at us. Beyond the great stone arch below we met my father in his deputy sheriff's car. He was out looking for us. He said Miss Eulalie had phoned till she found him. Miss Alexandria asked him to give the candy truck salesman ten dollars. Then we got into my father's car and were driven home.

Miss Eulalie met us in the hall.

"My stars, what happened to you, Alix! Your face is all blood. Fanny! Come quickly. I warned you, Alix, but you're like Jack, you wouldn't listen. I knew something would happen to him the time his ship was torpedoed. I warned him not to leave me but he said it was his duty. Only the mercy of God saved him. Fanny, call Dr. Howell and have him come right away. Jack lost everything but the uniform on his back, and that was ruined by sea water. He said he had bought a perfectly gorgeous kimono for me in Nagasaki embroidered in red and garnet and with magnificent loose sleeves. I never saw that one except in my dreams. Whenever the fourteenth of June comes around, I dream about that kimono at the bottom of the China Sea. Then I know Jack is near. He said it was a pale ivory and would have looked splendid on me. The colors would have gone so well with my hair and complexion. He got me another later but it wasn't the same."

All the time she spoke she was following Miss Alexandria upstairs. She tried to help her but Miss Alexandria threw off her hands. They disappeared into Miss Alexandria's room from which Miss Eulalie soon emerged on some errand for her cousin.

"Miss Alexandria wants to see you," she told me. I ran upstairs and found her sitting in a near state of collapse on the cushioned rattan armchair in the bay window.

"Open the window for me, Tommy," she said. "I must have some air or I'll expire. Thank you, child. Now go down to your father. Ask him to keep that woman out till the doctor comes. Even if he has to commit murder. If I hear once more about the kimono Jack bought her with the magnificent loose sleeves, I'll go stark-raving mad."

Fanny hurried in as I went out. The doctor came soon afterward. I told my father what Miss Alexandria had said. He informed Miss Eulalie that Miss Alexandria was hungry for sweet corn picked fresh off the stalk and he had promised to get some. Would she do him the favor of riding along out to the Spitler farm and selecting the nice young ears she thought Miss Alexandria would like.

My father made an excellent job of it, keeping Miss Eulalie away from the house for more than three hours, but that evening there was no help for it. Already on the stairs I could hear the two cousins at it. When I went by in the upstairs hall I saw Miss Alexandria propped up in bed, her face clear of blood but pale and pasted with strips of adhesive while Miss Eulalie went back and forth on the small cushioned maple rocker.

"You should have gone to the hospital like Dr. Howell said!" she reproached. "You wouldn't have had to take a step. I didn't when I went. They lifted me right up in one of those stretcher beds and I'm sure that big car of your undertaker would ride easy as a baby carriage. You wouldn't have minded it a bit."

"I would so have minded. I will not be put in a hearse while I'm still alive."

"It isn't a hearse. It's an ambulance."

"It's the same thing. You can hardly tell the difference. Then if they blew the hearse's fire alarm and drove like crazy with me closed up where I couldn't stop them, I'd die of spite and they'd have to turn around and bring me right back to Benny Stetler's cooling room."

"You're afraid of hospitals, Alix," Miss Eulalie accused.

"I'm afraid of nothing, especially not our own Chamber City hospital. Why, the Morleys helped to found it. I give generously to it every year as Father did before me. When they had me there with appendicitis, I had a wonderful time. Every evening my afternoon nurse would get me ready for bed. She'd turn off the light and sit there quiet till the night nurse came. Then my nice night nurse would close the door and turn on the lights, roll up the bed, make an alligator pear salad and we'd feast and talk till morning. You know, I can never go to sleep till after midnight anyhow. The interns and surgeons found out I had a party and would come in. I always had the nurse make cocktails for them and a special one for Dr. Heller who sewed me up. Jenny Yungling was in at the same time and would come up to see me. All in all I had a perfectly gorgeous time, and then you say I don't like hospitals. It shows how little you really and truly know about me, Eulalie.

"Well, you wouldn't go today for the doctor. He said you were probably hurt inside and they wouldn't know it if you didn't get X-rayed and put under observation."

"I'm under observation here," Miss Alexandria said acerbly. "I asked Fanny to stay tonight."

"What could Fanny and I do if you suddenly started to die. We couldn't give you shots to keep you alive. All we could do was ask how you'd like to look in your casket."

"Benny Stetler knows how I'd like to look. I told him to put it down on paper but if he forgot, it wouldn't matter much because I wouldn't know about it. Once they have me down at his place they can do with me what they like. I won't be any the wiser."

"You mean you're going to let them take you to some awful undertaking parlor and be viewed and all that?"

"Well, of course, I don't believe much in it. We never

did that in our day. It would be easier to let me be as I am and close the lid and let them look at that. But they expect it in this town. They want to look you over. I told Benny to go ahead and it would be all right."

"Alix! I don't see how you could do it."

"I won't have anything to do with it. They'll do it."

"But you could give your orders in advance. My nice undertaker in Sweetwater promised to do just as I say. I told him I hoped he wouldn't die before me like the other two did. He said he wouldn't. I have some material left from that gray dress my little dressmaker made for me years ago. I asked her if she'd keep the material and make me something like a robe. You know in the old days they had shrouds. I remember seeing men buried in black shrouds. But gray would be nicer and more cheerful."

"You're going to be buried in that?" Miss Alexandria's voice came thick with disgust.

"I think it would be lovely. I'm having Ellie May do my hair. She's done it for twenty years. I said to the undertaker, now don't get some strange woman to wash and brush my hair. Let Ellie May do it. He said he would. You could do the same with your nice Mrs. Somebody up the street."

"And scare the life out of Bessie! She's skittish enough. She's always telling me about her nerves. I tell her how to make them strong like mine. Did your hairdresser say she'd be willing to do it?"

"I didn't say anything to her yet. But I did talk to the undertaker. You know, I've seen some of my friends all rouged up in their casket and I told him I wouldn't want that to happen to me. I only hope if I go before you, you'll wear mourning for me, Alix. I've worn deep mourning four times, for Jack, for my mother and father, and for Aunt Lolly, but when Billy died, I didn't. I thought perhaps I'd done enough. But I would for you, Alix, if something happened to you tonight."

"I don't want you to wear deep mourning for me. You can wear anything you like. You wouldn't do what you said anyhow. You promised to give me that brooch of Grandmother's but you gave it to that namesake of yours who hasn't a drop of Fortune blood in her veins and yet you let her wind you around her finger."

"I gave you Grandmother's sewing chest of drawers, and I'll give you Grandmother's emerald locket if you promise to will it to Eulalie Smith when you die."

"No," Miss Alexandria said positively, "I won't. You gave me Grandmother's sewing chest of drawers because it was in your attic and you had no place to put it."

"That's a terrible thing to say, Alix. Especially when you're badly hurt and it might be the last thing I'd remember you said. It would make me feel very badly. You know I love you dearly, more than anybody else and it would make me happy to have you will me some of your things, especially Aunt Lolly's diamond ring and the Oriental rug at the end of your living room. I think you said it was a Bokhara. It would go so well with my Bokhara in Sweetwater."

"I'll do it if you write me a letter you'll give it to Hope when you die."

"You just said you wouldn't give our grandmother's locket to my Eulalie Smith and now you expect me to give your things to your Hope!"

"Hope is our own blood and your Eulalie Smith is just an interloper."

Miss Eulalie wiped her eyes.

"You hurt me, Alix. You do her an injustice. She comes in and helps me to decide what to do with my things. She's a comfort and peace of mind. Before that I had such problems. You know, everybody in my will kept dying and I had to change it and I changed it so often the bank got cross with me and that's really the main reason I never changed it for you."

"Every bank draws a long face about changing your will," Miss Alexandria said. "You have to be firm with them. When Mr. Lindley looks down his nose at me I tell him his bank had one slice out of the estate when Father died and another when Blanche died and they'd get a third when I was no longer here. How much do they want for writing a little piece of paper? Who's going to pay your inheritance tax, the trust company or your executors?"

"I never bother with such things, Alix. You and Eulalie Smith can decide and if you don't think I've treated you right you can sit down and talk it over together. I'm sure she'll let you have anything you want very bad, especially that you're one of the executors."

"By that time you'll have given everything away and you won't have a rocking chair left for me to sit on. I'm glad you can't give her your lot at Arlington or you wouldn't have any place to be buried in."

Miss Eulalie simpered, pleased.

"I'd still have plenty of place at Sweetwater, Alix. You know how the folks thought I simply had to be buried with the rest of the family. There was so much room and still is but Jack liked this lot at Arlington and you could buy one in those days. Now you can't. And they keep the lots at Arlington so perfect. You never need to cut the grass or trim around the stones. They're supposed to do that in Sweetwater, too, but they don't get around to it very often. Especially in a rainy year. Even if you have perpetual care. I still have Mother's lot and the Shapleigh lot and Grandfather's lot with half a dozen places where Jack and I could lie but he had his mind set on Arlington. He picked out a wonderful location. The road comes close and you have a grand view. It's really a choice place to be. I have a monument already put up for us. In those days they carved the wife's name on, too. They only left the date of her death blank because they didn't know what it would be. But then in World War One or Two so many airmen's wives married again after their names were carved on, so they didn't do it any more."

The Aristocrat

Here she was, at it again, going on about Arlington and there was no stopping her. I passed in the hall several times and saw her moving back and forward on the little rocker while Miss Alexandria lay in her bed still as death, her eyes closed. And so it went from Arlington to Portsmouth to Charlestown to Norfolk to Sweetwater and always back to her favorite house on Puget Sound.

"You know that's where I brought my things after Grandmother died. I put her tilt table under the west window. It was a perfect setting for it and the lamp I bought in Boston went beautifully there. Grandmother's rosewood table with the drawer that was so hard to open I put in the front window and below that the Kazak rug Jack bought for me in Beirut. Grandmother's china closet with the scrolled doors fitted perfectly in the second room. You could see it from the parlor with all Grandmother's green Wedgwood dishes that were made before the bombing so we could never get replacements for one or two pieces that are missing. But that made them all the more rare and valuable. On the top shelves were the Adam plates and the blue and white cups that George Washington drank out of when he was surveying the site for Washington City. Then I took the blue Mortimer pitcher I picked up at a sale in Sweetwater—"

At this point I said to heck with the blue Mortimer pitcher and closed the door to my room.

Chapter vii

Fanny didn't go home that night or for many days thereafter. When I came in the house during the evening, she met me in the downstairs hall.

"Miss Alexandria's worse. You better tell your father. I called the doctor and Miss Eulalie went for the minister."

I knew then it was serious. My father wasn't at home and I left word for him at the Miners' House. When I came up the stairs I heard Miss Eulalie's voice pleading in Miss Alexandria's room.

"You know I love you dearly, Alix. I'd never forgive myself if I let you go to the next world a heathen. We call you Alexandria but you were never really christened. You're like Grandmother's saddle horse, Dolly. We just called her that. It was all right for Dolly because she had no hope of heaven, but you have and it's a sin to turn your back on it."

"I don't turn my back on it at all," Miss Alexandria said with weary patience. "I've told you before how it was. Father, as you know, was Methodist to please Uncle Asa and Mother Reformed, and neither wanted to hurt the other's feelings by baptizing me in their own faith. Not only me but Hope and Blanche as well. That's why I always let it stand and Blanche did too. We didn't want to destroy their consideration for each other."

"That Catholic nurse of Blanche's didn't think it very considerate when Blanche died without being baptized. I saw her cry all through the funeral. She said it was the duty of a Catholic to baptize any dying person who wasn't baptized. She didn't know Blanche was unsanctified. She said she'd never be forgiven, and I'll never forgive myself if I let you go to the next world a heathen."

"Well, if it bothers you, you can baptize me yourself when I'm dying and unconscious and I won't know what you're doing."

"No, you can't put it on me, Alix. I'm not Catholic and you aren't either. We're Protestant and our minister has to do it. Now if it was something that took your strength like taking a bath or washing your hair, I wouldn't think of it, but all you need do is sit or lie there in bed, and let a minister splash a few drops of warm water on your head."

"Our Reformed minister's at synod or whatever you call it. I saw it in the *Miners' Journal*."

"Well, then I'm sure your good neighbor, Rev. Danner, would do it for you."

"No," Miss Alexandria said with finality. "It may be

all right for an infant but at my age it's ridiculous. I don't intend to have people laugh at me like they did at that old fool in *Life With Father*."

"He wasn't very old, if I remember, Alix. He was only half your age, and it gave him admission to heaven."

"How do you know he ever got there? The book didn't say so. The Bible doesn't say Abraham was ever baptized. I'm sure if St. Peter never was, he'd have sympathy for another poor soul who wasn't and let me in."

"St. Peter was a saint and you're not."

"I'm not an infant either," Miss Alexandria said tartly. "And I don't intend to act like one."

"The Bible says unless you're as a little child you can't enter the kingdom of heaven. You know Jack was never baptized either—not until we were married. I've thanked myself a thousand times since he's gone that I did that much for him. We didn't know then how close he was to heaven. He was only fifty-six, you remember. That was thirty years ago. Now you and I are old ladies."

"I'm not," Miss Alexandria interrupted her. "I'm not old and I won't be old. I'm just getting old. And I have no intention of going to heaven or anywhere else tonight."

"That's what Jack thought when he left us. He said he was just going to get forty winks. He told me all was well, not to worry. Everything would be better now."

"Maybe everything was better for him," Miss Alexandria said meaningly but it was lost on her cousin.

"I couldn't stand such a shock again, Alix. You remember we were living in that house on Puget Sound. I mean the house with Grandmother's things and the old rose and gold brocade drapes. I only wish you had come out to see those drapes, Alix. I had them made myself but the Navy paid for them. Jack saw to that. You know how those Navy houses are. This one especially needed something to dress it up. I was downtown shopping in Seattle when I saw the material. I knew at once it was for me. The trouble was there were two shades. One was old rose and the other gold. Both were brocades. I didn't know which I liked best so I bought them both and had a clever woman make them up. You can't imagine what they did for that house, the gold brocade in the dining room and the rose brocade in the parlor. Every soul that saw them complimented me. Even the sentry used to look in when he passed, though he's not supposed to. I told Jack and Jack said he was looking at me. Of course, he was looking at the drapes. Now I want to tell you just how they looked and how I hung them. We took—"

"Oh, oh, ooooh!" Miss Alexandria groaned.

"Alix. What's the matter? You're not leaving us?"

"Anything, anything," Miss Alexandria moaned.

"You mustn't, Alix. Don't do anything in a hurry. The doctor will be here soon. He still had a sick patient when I called. Rev. Danner's coming, too. He was out but Mrs. Danner said she would send him over the minute he came."

That brought Miss Alexandria around.

"Rev. Danner? What for?"

"Now don't ask me, Alix. It's all for your benefit. You've been badly hurt and can't be expected to do it for yourself."

"Do what?" Miss Alexandria demanded.

"You won't have to do anything. Rev. Danner will do it all. Mrs. Danner said he'd bring the silver fount he uses. Fanny has water on the stove so it won't give you a chill."

I saw Miss Alexandria's face. She reached for the bell button at the side of her bed, but Miss Eulalie was there ahead of her.

"What do you want, Alix? What can I do?"

"You can ring for Fanny and tell her to take that damned water off the stove. I am not going to have a baby."

"Now, Alix, be reasonable!" her cousin begged her but kept standing in the way so Miss Alexandria couldn't reach the button.

"Oh! Oh! Ooooh!" Miss Alexandria groaned again. "Why didn't I commit murder while I was young and able! Tommy! Will you please call Fanny?"

In a minute I had the maid at the door.

"Thank God, you're here, Fanny. Now don't leave me. I want you to stand by my side and protect me."

Fanny's face never changed. She was long used to curious instructions from her mistress. Besides, to Fanny as to my father, Miss Alexandria was never in the wrong. She moved to the side of the bed and stood there impassively. What might have happened then we'll never know because there was the sound of the distant front door. Presently the yellow hair of Dr. Howell appeared in the doorway.

"What's going on here?" he said cheerfully to Miss Alexandria, putting his medicine kit on a chair. "You've been misbehaving again," he joked and took her pulse. Then he drew his stethoscope from his pocket and listened to her heart and chest.

"How is she, Doctor?" Miss Eulalie begged.

He didn't answer but looked around.

"Where's the last medicine I left for her?"

"It was horrid," Miss Alexandria spoke up. "It made me feel dull as dishwater."

"You want to live, don't you?"

"I don't know," she said. "I haven't made up my mind yet."

He had Fanny get the medicine which she made a face over. The front door sounded again and presently the Rev. Danner, holding a silver fount and small black book, appeared in the doorway. Miss Alexandria, who had always welcomed him with gracious courtesy, now stared at him balefully.

"What's this?" Dr. Howell asked jocularly. I'm sure Miss Eulalie must have spoken to him about it when she phoned. "It looks like I'm just in time for a christening."

"I hope, Doctor, you'll stand by me and throw that thing out of the window," she said.

The doctor, who I knew was Catholic, grew grave.

"I think you better go ahead with it," he told her, and left.

Something died out of her face then and her eyes went around the room from one to another of the rest of us as if we were her enemies gathered here against her. Even I in the doorway felt included. But now the medicine Dr. Howell had given her began to have its effect. As if knowing opposition was useless, she rebelled outwardly no longer. She lay there pale and defiant while Fanny was sent into the bathroom for water. Then all took their positions while the voice of the Rev. Danner at the foot of the bed came out strong and commanding as I had heard it at a funeral only a few weeks before.

The only sign Miss Alexandria gave during the whole thing was when some water ran down her face and she dabbed at it viciously with her handkerchief. After the Rev. Danner finished, his face that had borne a kind of churchly holiness became human again. He shook her hand and spoke words of welcome.

Miss Alexandria looked from one to the other.

"Now it wasn't so bad, was it, Alix?" Miss Eulalie asked.

"It was a precious experience, I'm sure," the minister agreed. "I'm only glad I could do it for a friend and neighbor."

Miss Alexandria gave him a polite grimace.

"I suppose I must thank you, Rev. Danner, although I

didn't feel like a sinner before and don't feel any different now. But it was good of you to come over at such a late hour. You'll hear from me tomorrow for your trouble."

"Oh, that won't be necessary, Miss Alexandria," he said gallantly. "Of course, if you wish to make some personal gift, I'm sure that Mrs. Danner and I can use it. I'll be dropping in anyhow tomorrow to bring you the weekly contribution envelopes, now that you're a member."

There was a little dead silence. Miss Alexandria's smile had dissipated.

"A member? A member of what, Rev. Danner?"

"Why, of the great body of our church," he beamed. "Of the Lutheran church in general and our St. Matthew's in particular. In good standing, I should say," he added, very pleased as well he might be to have the wealthiest citizen of the town now a sheep of his flock and secure in the fold.

"I understood I was just to be baptized, Rev. Danner," she reminded him and under the politeness I could feel the steel. "I don't think you asked if I wished to become a member of your church?"

"The baptism of an adult automatically admits him to the brotherhood of the Lutheran church, Miss Alexandria," he explained.

"But I have no intention of becoming a Lutheran," she informed him. "I'm Reformed."

He looked startled.

"I was not so aware," he said slowly. "If you were Reformed, Miss Alexandria, you would already have been baptized, and you told me yourself sometime ago that you never were."

"I was never formally baptized," she agreed calmly. "But my mother was Reformed. My grandmother was Reformed and so were my ancestors back for hundreds of years before our American Revolution. It was always understood that I was to be Reformed."

The Rev. Danner was silent and plainly unhappy.

"I'm Reformed, Alix," Miss Eulalie said with satisfaction. "But you're Lutheran now."

"I'm not," Miss Alexandria announced. "I'll be no spiritual brother to Nell and Jenny's father. I couldn't abide him."

"But Rev. Danner just did it, Alix. He took you into the church when he baptized you."

"Then he'll have to baptize me out."

"He can't unbaptize you, Alix. He'd have to read you out of the church. You wouldn't want him to do that."

The Rev. Danner managed agreement. I thought I caught a fleeting glimpse of relief that he was not to have the prize snatched from his grasp and given to a rival.

"There's really not too much difference between the major denominations today, Miss Alexandria. Ecumenicalism is the modern watchword. Soon, I think, we'll all be one grand body, the Methodists and Reformed or Church of Christ as they call themselves now, the Presbyterians, the Lutherans, and the Catholics. Indeed some say that Catholics are becoming more Lutheran and we Lutherans more Catholic every day."

"I wouldn't object to being a Catholic again," Miss Alexandria told him firmly. "We were all Catholics back before the Reformation. But my mother refused to be anything but Reformed and my mind is made up like hers."

The clergyman gazed at her in uncertainty. It was plain he didn't know quite what to do.

"I think you'll feel better after a night's rest, Miss Alexandria," he said soothingly. "You had a very bad accident. We are all thankful you weren't killed outright. Tomorrow I'll come over and instruct you in our catechism. I'm sure you'll be glad that after all these long years you've finally been given baptism and admitted to membership in the Christian church. We're so convenient, just across the street, and there's a special service to interest you next Sunday. I'm preaching on baptism and what it means. I hope now that you're one of my members, you'll be able to come and hear me."

She gazed at him a long moment in dangerous silence.

"Very well, Doctor Danner," she said, and I knew by the title that he had better look out. "But I shall never forgive the Lutherans for shanghaiing me like this. Since I must now willingly or unwillingly be a member of your church, I shall come to hear you next Sunday. And since I can't read your lips when you stand so high in that pulpit of yours, I'll ask Martin to bring a stepladder up in front for me to sit on."

The minister drew back. He looked hastily at Miss Eulalie as if to ask, is this one of your cousin's little jokes? He found only alarm on Miss Eulalie's face.

"You really wouldn't, Alix," she protested. "You wouldn't embarrass Rev. Danner like that?"

"You know me, Eulalie; I generally pay my debts," she said grimly. "Good night, Doctor Danner. You may go, too, Eulalie, and heat your warm milk you say you can never get to sleep without. If Fanny is still up, will you call her back to get me ready for bed?"

The clergyman and Miss Eulalie left, not at once but eventually, and I did too. When I awoke during the night I could see in my mind Miss Alexandria perched on a high stepladder between the Rev. Danner's pulpit and the congregation. I remembered now hearing of other un- likely things she had done. She had told the Reformed pastor that the stained-glass window in memory of her mother was the ugliest thing she had ever seen. And when her trained nurse made some disparaging remarks against grand opera, Miss Alexandria, a devout opera fan, had made her sit and listen to grand opera on the radio all Saturday afternoon.

I saw that Miss Eulalie was really worried. The Rev. Danner when he came next day tried anxiously to appease which only added to the pale determination in Miss Alex- andria's eyes. Sunday morning I woke with a sense of gathering apprehension in the house. At ten thirty, a most unusual hour for her, I saw Miss Alexandria descend the stairs dressed in one of the dark silks she wore on formal occasions.

Miss Eulalie cringed at the sight of her.

"Surely, Alix!" she begged. "Surely you've forgiven Rev. Danner?"

"I've forgiven but not pardoned him," she said serenely. "I fully expected to visit his church this morning. That is, if I hadn't been dizzy on getting up. Fanny and I both thought I might fall off the stepladder and that would be slightly ridiculous. So I decided to visit my own Reformed church instead. I hope you and Tommy will go along for moral support."

With relief Miss Eulalie agreed, scurrying upstairs to get herself ready while I ran over to tell my father to take out the car. When I got back, Miss Eulalie hadn't as yet come down. She did finally. Miss Alexandria had me take her smelling salts, atomizer, Dr. Howell's medicine and two bright red pillows.

"The Reformed are a very hardy race," she explained. "Mother always complained of having to sit on her bones. But I refuse to in church. It arouses blasphemous thoughts in my mind."

We made, I thought, a curious party getting out of the car in front of the church. My father had to double park on the far side of the street and stand with his deputy sheriff badge stopping all traffic so the two old ladies could manage to climb out and cross to the church while I followed loaded with the red cushions, medicine, smelling salts and the atomizer.

The congregation was singing a hymn as we entered. I thought people looked at us queerly but Miss Alexandria led her imperious way up to what had been her mother's pew in the front where I arranged the red cushions for her, one beneath her and one at her back. Once settled, she duly opened her hymn book from the rack but before she could find the place, the singing stopped, the congregation rose, I with them, while the two ladies kept to their seat. The preacher began speaking with his arms extended. I found to my dismay he was giving the benediction.

I glanced at Miss Alexandria wondering what she would do now. I had no need for misgiving. Although she could hear nothing of the organ bursting forth in joyful relief now that the solemnities were over, she could see the others starting to leave and I'm sure sensed what had happened. Unperturbed she rose and graciously greeted those near her together with older members who came up to shake hands and tell her how glad they were to see her in her mother's church. Indeed it turned into a small but gay and triumphant party there amid the pews with Alexandria chatting warmly to all, bowing and smiling and introducing her cousin to those who didn't know her, while I stood behind her loaded with her medicine, smelling salts, the atomizer and her bright red cushions.

Chapter viii

ALL SUMMER the Primrose Coal Company kept its colliery shut down, its office windows boarded up and its men out of work. It would never open again, everyone said. But Miss Alexandria stood firm.

"They think a woman will wilt," she told Fanny. "They don't know what pine knots we Morleys are."

At the first spell of fall weather, Mr. January came with papers to sign. The coal company had decided to reopen, he said. Taxes were paid, Miss Alexandria reimbursed, the office windows unboarded and the Primrose name added to the daily radio and *Miners' Journal* announcement of collieries working on the morrow. It was a great relief to my father, perhaps a secret one to Miss Alexandria. She never admitted it, only went around with her infallible face as if she knew all the time they would come around as soon as cool weather stiffened the hard coal market.

Now my father drove her up on Broad Mountain without incident. She forgave Rev. Danner's transgression, received him evenings in the library as of yore where they talked until midnight of Europe, the Mediterranean and the Holy Land. Although she never to my knowledge entered his church she mailed him a monthly check toward his salary. The monstrosity of the apartment house next door was finally finished. It turned out to have an attractive brick design in front, once the disorder of construction was gone. Best of all, Miss Eulalie along with a half hundred bundles and belongings returned to her home in Maryland. My father said she talked steadily all the hundred and fifty miles to Sweetwater. Afterward Miss Alexandria went to bed and stayed for a week.

"It's a family eccentricity," she told the doctor when he came. "All the Morleys had it. My father went through the Civil War on his nerve all the way from Bull Run to Gettysburg. Like I did with Eulalie. A bullet grazed his ear at Shiloh but he never allowed deafness to afflict him until he took off his uniform."

The doctor looked at me curiously. He probably knew as I did that, war or no war, most of the local Morleys were deaf in their later years. At the end of the week Miss Alexandria left her bed to come down for dinner but Fanny told my father she was not the same. We couldn't see it at first. She put up a show of her old gusto, banging doors and windows, sounds which never reached her ears. When my father forgot to take one of the window screens to the attic for the winter, she picked it up herself and ran it in that vigorous way of hers up the several flights of stairs. One cold day I came home to find her in the cellar determinedly shovelling coal.

"You might inform your father we are not Esquimaux," she said, handing the shovel to me.

My father kept the house a degree or two warmer after that. She had him take her to her dentist in Chamber City to have a tooth filled. "Next time I come," she told the dentist, "I'll have Martin bring a comfortable chair for me to sit on." She surprised us by going with an old friend, Mrs. Thompson, to see a play in New York. My father drove them to Harrisburg and carried their bags into the station.

"What!" she told the astonished young man at the ticket window. "All these years you've never paid me a penny dividend on my six hundred shares of Pennsylvania Railroad and now you want to charge me forty-eight dollars for just two tickets and a drawing room to New York!"

She went to bed for a week when she came back, but had me bring up a girl I knew at high school who called to sell her a subscription to the school paper. Miss Alexandria talked to her all evening.

"She's fabulous, simply fabulous!" the girl told me at the door.

I knew what she meant. She had seen the old Miss Alexandria who didn't live in Unionville at all but in quite another world, a very old and superior world, compounded of her family, memories and friends she once had, and of the house she still ruled, of the way she sat in her dressing gown on a chair in her bedroom and graciously entertained you, of the incredibly sage look she gave from her naked eyes when taking off her glasses for a moment to polish them, and of the personage she became when she would lay back her head and close her eyes for a moment, while her nose grew narrower, more aloof and overweening so that I, who had often seen her like this, wondered how the commonalities of modern life could ever reach high enough to lay serious hold of her.

Little did I realize then what lay ahead, the low means the wave of the future would choose to bring her down. Of the seasons, Miss Alexandria loved winter best, when pollen-bearing abominations were dead and the blessed frost covered the ground. Daily now I could see her at her library or bedroom desk playing endless solitaire or writing letters in a thin shaken hand changed from the flying strokes and forceful twists when I had been younger. When it snowed she sat at the window watching it fall on her trees and shrubs, exclaiming to Fanny or my father or me to come and see what she saw. Other times she read the *Miners' Journal*, the Philadelphia *Inquirer* and the Sunday *Times* or paged restlessly through the host of magazines she took and which she had Fanny keep in methodically laid smooth-paper shingles on her library table.

When all else failed, she sat at a front window and watched with heightening disbelief the unending stream of traffic.

"You say I'm lucky I can't hear it," she told my father. "I can feel it in my bones, especially the trucks. If they bothered me as much as they do you, I'd go out in the middle of the street and stop them and send the drivers back where they belong."

My father said he wouldn't put it past her, but I think the traffic stimulated rather than offended her. She might in her old age be confined to this Anthracarbona County town she happened to be born in, but her house still had a window on the world, and more than once when she couldn't sleep she told me next morning she had sat in her dressing gown at a back upstairs window and watched the car lights come over the Blue Mountain.

"They're beautiful like winter fireflies," she said. "Now you see them and now you don't."

No, it wasn't the trucks that brought her down in the end but something more hellish, to use one of her own favorite words. Late one morning my father came in the library to ask if there was anything more he could do.

"Nothing, Martin, thank you," she told him. "Wait. Yes, there is. The last night or two I thought I detected a very unpleasant odour in my bedroom. It came from the window and was still there in the morning when Fanny closed it. I asked her but she didn't seem to know. Have you any idea what it could be?"

My father's eyes strayed to Fanny standing mute and troubled in the dining room doorway.

"I'll look into it, Miss Alexandria, and let you know if I find out."

"No, you'll find out now, Martin, and tell me right away. It's very disagreeable. It smells as if this rabbit warren next door burns its garbage at night."

My father hesitated. It was plain neither he nor Fanny wanted to speak about it.

"I don't think it's the apartment house, Miss Alexandria," he said reluctantly.

"Well, who is it then? Such smells and smoke don't come of themselves."

My father looked unhappy.

"It isn't anybody in particular. It's the dump."

Miss Alexandria turned a freezing face toward him.

"Did you say, dump? Whose dump and where is it that it comes in my bedroom window?"

My father gave a despairing look at Fanny who bolted. I could hear her go through the pantry door.

"It's the town dump, Miss Alexandria. In the old canal. The town council's made a dump out of it."

"What are you trying to tell me, Martin?" she said, sharply. "You know as well as I do that the canal's Morley property. It always has been. Grandfather bought it when the canal company disbanded. He paid taxes on it all his life. My father paid taxes on it all his life and I paid taxes until the Civic Organization wanted it for a town park. They said then I wouldn't have to pay any more taxes. They came to see me, that minister who was at the head of it, and the lawyer I call the Chewing Gum man. They said the canal was starting to smell and they'd make it into a beautiful town park."

"I know, Miss Alexandria," my father nodded sadly. "They never got very far with it. They claimed it took too much money. Last winter they gave the canal to the town council and the council voted to make it a dump."

Miss Alexandria was staring at him.

"Will you please go to my telephone, Martin, and call Mr. January. Tell him I must see him right away."

My father went to the door, hesitated and came back.

"I better tell you, Miss Alexandria, that Mr. January knows about it. I told him when I first heard what was going on. He and the bank always said not to upset you with anything but to come to them. Mr. January called me back. He said there was nothing he could do. He said you had sold them the canal legally. He said they gave you a dollar and you signed their agreement without asking him about it and when he found out, it was too late to do anything. He told me not to tell you what he said till you asked about it."

Scorn was rising on Miss Alexandria's face.

"I always said that pair could never be trusted, the

Methodist minister and the Chewing Gum man. I know
now why he wrote the agreement himself and was in such
a hurry for me to sign it. I've heard he's building his own
house far from the smoke, in Dumont. And I don't thank
you and Mr. January and Mr. Nolan for keeping this
from me as if I were a senile old woman. Now will you
go to my telephone, Martin, and tell Mr. January I want
to see him."

Mr. January came the next afternoon. I couldn't hear
what was said but Miss Alexandria's pale face at supper
told me some. She had my father invite the borough
council members and they came at her summons to drink
her highballs and get a look at the inside of the Morley
house. They listened silently to what she had to say of the
evils of air pollution, of her own increased asthma attacks
and of the long tradition of clean pure air in Unionville
which in her youth, she declared, smelled only of pines
and the healthful aroma of hemlock and rock oak bark
from the tanyard. But they made no promises. Afterward
I heard two were for her and the rest against. One asked,
why doesn't she keep her window closed? Another said
a dying old woman couldn't stand in the way of progress
—by the time the town got a new dump site, she'd be in
the cemetery.

Dr. Kurtz, the old health officer, stood with them,
egged them on.

"It's a fad, all this fuss about air pollution," he told
them. "Look at Philadelphia. All those people are still

alive, aren't they? Any butcher knows that smoke cures meat, doesn't spoil it."

Dr. Howell was of another opinion. He tried to get Miss Alexandria away for her asthma's sake, to go to the shore or mountains. "Most people don't have the means. You do," he told her but she bowed her Morley back.

"I won't desert my people. Those three houses facing the canal were the first piece of property Father owned. Grandfather gave them to him. What do you think my tenants go through every night down there? And all their children!"

"The mayor says nobody's complained except you and I and the wife of the chemistry teacher at the high school."

"I know her," Miss Alexandria said, meaning she had heard of her. "She comes from Wisconsin or Maine or some state up there. She's not Pennsylvania Dutch. Oh, the Pennsylvania Dutch have their good points. All the miners at Father's and Uncle Asa's colliery were Pennsylvania Dutch. Then the Europeans started coming in. I love Europe and Europeans but on Christmas they'd buy a case of whisky for their inside boss, so he'd give them an easy place to dig coal. The Pennsylvania Dutch never did that. They'd cut off a hand sooner than bribe or flatter. I know all about them. I'm Pennsylvania Dutch myself."

"With a name like Morley?" the doctor jeered.

"Well, I'm part Pennsylvania Dutch anyway. Grandmother Morley was a Stout from Berks County. What does that make me, a quarter or something? Her father had flour mills and brought Grandfather Morley a fine dowry. That's what he built his fortune on. I can feel her in my blood sometimes. She doesn't like me to speak out. You know, you could never hold a New England town meeting among the Pennsylvania Dutch. Only a few of us hardy souls would come. The rest would stay home. It's born in them, come down from their ancestors. For generations in Germany they were under the yoke. Even brides had to spend the first night with their baron. When some came to America, Father told me, they wouldn't lift a finger against the Indians that massacred their families. 'It's God's will,' they said."

"I've heard some people in this town speak out," the doctor said dryly.

"You've heard me. But you never heard Willy Kimmel. His mother lived all her life in one of my houses. I still get him in to open my drains. I said to him one time, 'William, I hear that new woman in my house next door to you has another man living with her. They say he got drunk last week and threw a chair through one of my windows. Now I don't care about the window but I wonder if my tenants ever bother you.' Willy looked away. 'I don't know anything about it, Miss Alexandria,' he said. He wouldn't talk. He didn't want to get involved. It might hurt his business or his neighbor relations. That's why almost nobody in Germany stood up against that mad man, Hitler. I guess I'd have been shot. It's the only way to keep a Morley quiet."

"Your asthma would be better if you followed your Pennsylvania Dutch grandmother," the doctor said.

"It would be deadly," she dismissed it. "I'd never forgive myself and St. Peter wouldn't either. Don't forget he cut off the high priest's servant's right ear."

Miss Alexandria never gave up. She made life miserable for the town council. She had my father argue for her at council meetings and when he begged off, she attended herself against Dr. Howell's orders, harassing the councilmen who didn't know what to do with her gracious Morley superiority and icy rejoinders. She wrote the governor, whose mother she had known, and when she had only a polite note from a secretary indicating that he didn't want to become involved, she polished her glasses, the old imperious look came to her high thin nose and she wrote a letter in her spidery patrician hand to the local *Weekly Luminary*. How they deciphered it, I don't know, but it was duly printed and brought a quick note of praise from the high school chemistry teacher's wife. Several people including two minority council members, stopped me on the street and told me to tell Miss Alexandria they agreed with her. It was all the encouragement she needed to let herself go. She wrote another letter, this one castigating her own political party which controlled the council. It was reprinted in the county seat *Miners' Journal*. A reporter was sent to town to interview her.

The story that came out of it, my father said, greatly disturbed the county politicos. It also made the majority of our town council very unhappy. He said they and the county seat men were putting their heads together to see how to stop her.

"They'll do something but they'll never gag Miss Alexandria," my father predicted.

The news of what they did broke first in the *Miners' Journal*, then in the local *Luminary*. The report was that Dr. Kurtz had resigned because of age, and the town council with state approval was offering the post of Unionville health officer to Miss Alexandria Morley.

"It's a trick," my father said. "They know a lady like her could never take it. And if she doesn't, then she can't complain any more."

Dr. Howell treated it as a joke.

"It's a bit ridiculous but I'm afraid they've put one over on you, Miss Alexandria. I hope you know when you're licked and are ready for Atlantic City now."

"You don't think of taking it, Miss Alexandria?" Fanny begged.

"She couldn't do the job," Dr. Howell said. "She'd have to visit every restaurant and bar in town and see that the help washed their hands before they came out of the toilets."

"I like that," Miss Alexandria said. She was all set up to be the center of attention once more. "I've always wanted to tell certain people they needed a bath."

"You'd also," the doctor went on grimly, "have to inspect the toilets yourself. The men's as well as the women's."

"You make it sound more interesting. I've never seen the inside of men's lavatories before. Have you, Fanny?"

"Of course, you're not serious, Miss Alexandria," Dr. Howell said. "If you were, I'd have to come right out and forbid it. You'd be a candidate for a heart attack on your first rounds."

"That's the best reason for dying at my age I've heard," she told him, delighted, and none of us could tell whether or not she meant it. "They might even put a flag on my grave like on Father's. It would be almost like dying for your country."

Chapter ix

OWN COUNCIL was baffled, my father said, when
Miss Alexandria accepted. Fit to be tied, was the expression he used.

"They thought they had her fast," he told me, "but
they don't know her like I do." The word, council, is
plural in Unionville.

Not that this in any way settled the matter. Miss Alexandria smiled graciously on Solly Mengel in charge of the
dump and asked him to stop burning cartons and paper.
Councilman Minnichbach told him to pay no attention
and a majority of council backed him up. Not the one to
engage with her inferiors, Miss Alexandria wrote the
Secretary of Health at Harrisburg in her hieroglyphical
hand, naming various Morley credentials. When she
didn't hear in the next mail or two, she asked Fanny to
get his office on long distance whereupon she had her say
in no uncertain terms over the telephone, able to hear
nothing in return and never halting until she hung up.

Whom she reached and what the astonished listener thought, we never knew but several days later the district engineer for the health department appeared at the front door looking cautious and very curious. Presently I could hear him laughing in the library. No doubt she amused him. Certainly there must have been few like her among the general run of small town health officers.

The district engineer went from Miss Alexandria to the dump, then to the mayor, ordered the burning stopped, the acres of rotten accumulation of garbage covered with ground and the process to be repeated at the end of each dumping day. At the next council meeting, my father said, there was hell to pay. The opposing majority declared they never could get enough ground or pay for a bulldozer to move it, but in the end the decree prevailed, smoke stopped drifting into Miss Alexandria's window at night, her asthma attacks somewhat declined and a serene and impenetrable armor possessed her even, my father said, on her kitchen and toilet inspections where he took her in the car.

Somewhere I have come on a line of verse that takes me back to this particular time. It sounds like Shakespeare but who wrote it I really don't know, only that after reaching the scene of battle,

"Richard was himself again."

That was Miss Alexandria at this time. The polluters of her home town had been put in their place. She was again the gladiator swinging a golf club in the framed photograph that still hung in Miss Blanche's room. She had gained three pounds, she told us. Of late years, food had been an anathema to her. Eggs, she insisted, made her bilious, cabbage poisoned her blood, milk formed indigestible curds in her stomach and even crackers were unfit for anything except autointoxication. If it hadn't been for tea and toast, she used to say, she would have evaporated into thin air. Now she sat in her dining chair more or less content and ate most everything from the menu she dictated daily to Fanny. She still would touch no milk, declaring it fit only for babes who had nothing better to do than scream with colic, although of late she took second helpings of ice cream from the cut-glass dish that Fanny held at her elbow.

"I'm not inconsistent," she insisted to the doctor. "I simply recognize the facts of life. I like people individually but not the public. Beware of anyone, Doctor, who says he loves people but not individuals. I wouldn't trust him with my dog or cat."

Miss Alexandria to my knowledge never had a dog or cat but now she had many callers. One was the Rev. Danner's earnest Sunday School superintendent who collected antiques and came to ask her counsel. He had had a letter from the Schuyler estate lawyer that he must return the old broken drop leaf cherry table Miss Jennie Schuyler had given him before she died. Meanwhile he had repaired it, scraped off seven coats of paint and refinished it in its natural color.

"Must I give it back, Miss Alexandria?" he begged her. She gave him a worldly wise and pitying smile.

"If you do, child, you should have your head examined. I should like to hear anyone tell me I had to give back what Miss Jennie gave me. I'd put him through his paces. You mustn't be scared by Mr. Carpenter. He's a charming man and stands very high as a lawyer and the only reason he wrote like that to you, I feel sure, is because the Schuylers' Cousin Eleanor forced him to. I know her. I know all about her. She's close to eighty if she's a day. What she wanted another drop leaf table for at her age I can't imagine. That's the time to start giving things away. She's also quite hard of hearing and demanding. I don't think it's being hard of hearing that makes her demanding. I'm not demanding, am I?"

"Why, I don't think so, Miss Alexandria," Mr. Hassler stammered.

"My cousin Hallie is both but I always took it to be pure coincidence. And the fact that she's very short like Miss Eleanor Fitzgibbon. Short people must make up for it some way. She was born and raised in Boston of Irish immigrant stock on her father's side and claims to be related to the Cabots or Lowells or somebody or other up there. She and the Schuyler girls never got along."

"She's very rich, they say." The Sunday School superintendent looked troubled.

"Very rich and proud. She didn't mind showing Miss Jennie and Miss Nell she looked down on them. Of course, the Schuyler girls had their limitations. They never drank or smoked. They wouldn't allow poker or roulette or champagne in their house, all the things I've been brought up on. They utterly refused to play cards for money, not even for pennies. Now the Morleys have drank and gambled and danced in their houses since the beginning of time."

The Sunday School superintendent looked a little bewildered but nodded manfully. Miss Alexandria went on.

"When Eleanor Fitzgibbon came to town one summer to visit her cousins, I thought I'd show her we weren't entirely uncivilized. So I invited her and Miss Jennie and Miss Nell to dinner. Fanny and I went to the pantry for our best things. Fanny enjoyed it as much as I. We hadn't dressed a table like that since Princess Vershaliv and the Eugene DuPonts came to this house, the best Morley silver, crystal and linen with every fork, knife, spoon and glass in its proper place. It seemed like old days. I can still see the Boston lady's face when she came out into the dining room and saw the table with the white candles burning and Fanny in a freshly laundered uniform standing by my chair. Fanny's Polly was in the kitchen. All my tradesmen friends had conspired with me. Joe at Stowell's in Philadelphia had ransacked the entire wholesale district for the best filets he could find. Tony at the Marsella Fruit Company had sent perfect artichokes. Fanny poured the Julien from the bottle on its side in its basket and all through dinner I dropped what hints I could to Miss Eleanor Fitzgibbon how we did things in Union-ville."

The Sunday School superintendent looked impressed yet baffled.

"But, Miss Alexandria. What should I do about the table and the letter from the Schuyler lawyer?"

"Burn it," she said. "I mean the letter. Then sit at your drop leaf table and drink champagne to celebrate."

"What if the sheriff comes with a search warrant?"

"He won't, child," she said reassuringly. "But if it makes you feel any better, you and Martin can bring the table up here and store it till things blow over. Really and truly, Edward, the sheriff of Anthracarbona County, knows better than to force his way into this house. If he does, I'll put him through his paces. Of course, you had better put a tag on the table saying it's your property. You know, against all that," she added, waving a hand toward the cemetery.

Nothing, so far as I know, ever happened to the table but something did to Hope. She came on one of her visits, bringing a youngish, likable fellow who stayed over the weekend, sleeping in the Mormon bed while Hope as usual occupied Miss Blanche's room. He left late Sunday afternoon to get to his work as a junior stock broker in Baltimore Monday morning, and already at the supper table Miss Alexandria started tactfully to draw her out on her young man, what he did, who his people were, how she had met him and whether she had any intention of marrying him. To Miss Alexandria, a man had no choice in the matter.

I could see Hope full of things to tell but she hesitated, glancing at me. Miss Alexandria looked tolerantly at her.

"You can say anything in front of Tommy, child. He knows all about us. It's like saying it under the rose bush. He never tells. He's a Morley, too, you know."

Hope was still not satisfied but she might well have been. What she told Miss Alexandria bored me. It was so like the sticky romantic confidences between girls at school, the same inexplicable emotion and excitement over boys. She named three men who had paid her address, a young Philadelphia clergyman, the fair-haired stock broker from Baltimore, and, lately, the yellow-haired Dr. Howell in Unionville. She couldn't make up her mind which to encourage. After listening knowingly, Miss Alexandria proceeded to enlighten her. It struck me as amusing to hear someone whom people in Unionville called an old maid confidently instructing a young girl in the facts of courtship and marriage.

"Now, of course, child, you're a Morley and will do as you like," she said. "But I'd sin against heaven if I didn't advise you never to enter an unholy alliance with a minister. I know all about ministers, child. We've had them come into this house all our lives. Uncle Timothy and Aunt Lou used to spend two months with us every summer. He was a D.D., L.L.D., and was sure he had his license straight from heaven. The greatest trial a wife can have, child, is a husband who thinks himself the right hand of God Almighty. He used to ask the blessing for ten minutes while everything on our table got cold. Mother told him three minutes were enough for anybody but he wouldn't remember. I seldom heard Father give the blessing but one day he got tired of Uncle Timothy and started in before Uncle got going. Both were deaf and kept on praying against each other while the rest of us wanted to roll under the table. When Father looked up triumphantly, Uncle Timothy was still at it. No, child, cast your net on the other side of the ship."

"My young minister is very nice, Alexandria," Hope said.

"Ministers," Miss Alexandria pronounced, "have the devil's own attraction for females. I never understood why. Now physicians don't. I suspect girls are a bit scared of all those drugs including arsenic that a doctor could put in your coffee when you're not looking. Not that I'd marry a doctor myself but it wouldn't be for that reason. I'd simply have no patience sitting at home alone while he stayed up all night with a contrary woman who decided to have her baby when we were going out to dinner or the theater. If you think it would be nice to have a doctor in the house to look after your health, child, you're stark-raving mad. Ned's wife used to tell me he never had the time to take her blood pressure or even look at her tongue. It's about that bad with me. When Dr. Howell gets here on his Monday morning call, Martin sees him first outside and gets something for his ailments, then Fanny stops him in the front hall and has him give her pills for her feet and back. If Eulalie is here, she ties him up for half an hour with what she thinks is wrong with her. I have to pay for it all, but by the time he gets to me, he can just say good morning and run."

"Dr. Howell's never in a hurry with me. I think he's very nice."

"Lovely, lovely," Miss Alexandria agreed. "I'm devoted to him and he's devoted to me. But you didn't see him at the beginning. I've broken him in. He's learned a little about good manners and the way of life in a gentlewoman's house. I can even speak my mind to him now without him rushing out and slamming the door. Uncle Asa used to do that to Mother. One time he slammed it so hard he broke the transom. Next day he sent a man to fix it and after that he listened and said, 'Yes, Lolly,' and 'no, Lolly.' Dr. Howell's the same way. When I tell him his clothes look awful, he knows it's gospel and does something about them. Only last winter I said, don't ever come in this house with that awful black suit again, you look like an undertaker, and he never did. Now when he has beautiful clothes on, I ask him where he got that good-looking suit or tie."

"Isn't that good that he takes criticism?"

"It's good, but a man won't from his wife. He will from me, I can say anything to most anybody. I told Richard before he died I hoped he wouldn't get one of those ugly black tombstones like the rest of his family. If Tess had said it, he'd have jumped up out of his death bed. They always fought like dogs and cats and no wonder. All the things I know about their marriage. Some woman at Bessie's beauty parlor said to me once it was too bad I never had children. I settled her. I told her my childlessness was fully premeditated—I didn't intend to give birth to any prodigy I'd have to smirk over and brag about. I've never forgotten how bitterly disappointed Uncle Rob was in his four girls, especially Imogene and Lil. Uncle Rob was crazy about horses like all the Morley men, and none of his girls would ride or drive. I think it killed him in the end, he loved horses so. Did I ever tell you the time he held up the Lebanon train? He used to ride his mare, Gypsy, down to his farm every day and the railroad was the shortest way. One time he was late and the Lebanon train came up behind him. The engineer blew and blew but Uncle Rob was deaf as a post. The train had to crawl behind him until the engineer could send the fireman up on foot to pull at Uncle Rob's coat tails. Uncle Rob looked around. 'Well, Gypsy, we'll have to give precedence to quantity over quality,' he said. He told me more than once he'd have given an arm if one of his children could harness or unharness a horse like me."

Hope remained uncertain as had the Sunday School superintendent before her.

"I still don't know which one you'd advise me to marry, Alexandria."

"I never give advice, child. Especially not on marriage. I can't forget it was I who introduced Tess Morris to Richard. She was my roommate at Mrs. Somers' school. I thought I knew her. But, oh, oh, oh! what I found out after they were married. No, you must decide for yourself. Every man has his drawbacks. You'll want to poison him no matter whom you marry. But if I did give advice, I'd say, don't reject your young stock broker too quickly. He's Southern and you're Southern. He'll understand you and you will him. Southern men and Southern women have a certain way about them. Maybe you've noticed they always have something wrong with them. Even Uncle Sam, and he was indestructible. Jack took him one time to the Lambs Club in New York and John Barrymore and a few others tried to drink this back country plantation owner under the table. He drank them under instead. And yet, ask Uncle Sam how he was and he'd say, tolerable, just tolerable, like Eulalie. It's their disposition. It serves a purpose."

I thought as I ate Fanny's inimitable egg custard that although Miss Alexandria didn't realize it, she was drawing a perfect picture of herself.

"I still don't know which one you like," Hope repeated.

"Really and truly, child, liking has nothing to do with a happy marriage. Only the poor immature things raised on democracy like to think so. But there's one thing. Married to your young Maryland stock broker, you'd probably have to do what you wouldn't have to with the other two. I mean go to football games. I never could see the sense of watching young men pile on top of each other and then get carried off the field in a stretcher. Yet every winter before Richard was married, I'd have to go with him and Jack and sit on the Navy side and whoop and holler like I was crazy and all the time never knowing what I was whooping about."

Hope stayed for three or four weeks and Miss Alexandria treated her with the special consideration of those very near to her. In telling about someone prominent or nice, she would say, "She was just about as tall as you, Hope, and had your fair coloring." When it concerned an object Hope had some connection with, it would be, "Your Baltimore" or "your Hawaii" or "your father's army."

The last week it was something else.

"I'm sorry, child, to put you through a performance before you go. But perhaps you should know about relatives. Your young stockbroker from the South must have them. Southerners always have scads of kin. You'll have to live with them, you know."

"Oh, I'm not afraid of getting along with relatives, Alexandria. People like me."

"People, yes. God made people. But poor bungling man makes relatives and nearly always regrets it. I must tell you, child, I've had to invite your cousin, Hallie, for her birthday. She was an only child, you know, and never learned to take care of herself. I think that's why her marriage never worked out. We always thought Homer Jones a lamb. Opposites usually get together. But one day he was gone. I think he turned up in Iowa or Arizona or some place later on. Hallie never forgave him. She changed her name from Mrs. Homer Jones back to Mrs. Hallie Morley."

"I think I remember her," Hope said.

"You must. For years we had her here for Sunday dinner. That's when she still lived in Uncle Caleb's big white house above the head of the canal. She didn't have much money and by the middle of the week I'd start worrying about her and send Martin or Fanny with a chicken breast or slab of roast. And the next Sunday I'd have to sit at my own dinner table and hear her tell that the chicken was starting to spoil and that's why I sent it or that I never came to see her but made her come here to see me. It was hellish. A few years ago Rev. Danner got her into a private home. It's the house of the man whose father had been in the timber business with Uncle Caleb. They say at last she gets three meals a day and is happy. You remember her?"

"I don't think she ever liked me, Alexandria."

Miss Alexandria gave a wry smile.

"I see you remember her, child. She still won't read lips or wear a hearing aid. I'm asking Dr. Howell in for dessert. First, he wouldn't forgive me for not having him while you're here. And then it may be wise to have a physician handy. We'll all be buried on the same lot yet her father never paid a dollar toward it. Did I ever tell you about her mother, Aunt Liddy? She was very provident, always brought more home from Sunday School picnics than she took. Once a year she gave a party. She wouldn't be in sight to receive us when we came. About twenty of us would take hands and dance down the hall and parlor till we were exhausted. Then Aunt Liddy would appear, every year in a different costume and made up so we hardly knew her. Her refreshments were delicious. She made a wonderful almond-flavored cake. It was on the heavier side like a pound cake. Cousin Lucy and Aunty Ruby would say, 'I wonder if Aunt Liddy's going to give a party this year. I can hardly wait to taste that Vermont cake of hers.' "

Late Sunday morning, Miss Alexandria sent my father over the mountain with the car. I had a taste of what we were in for when I answered the door and found the guest there. She had been a lively, beautiful girl, Miss Alexandria said, with golden hair. Now she was deaf and lame. She came into the hall and looked at me suspiciously, then at Miss Alexandria who had stepped out from the library to welcome her.

"Your chauffeur wanted me to walk right in, Alix, but I refused. Not when I hadn't been invited to your house for two or three years."

Miss Alexandria, perhaps knowing her answer would

be unheard, just bowed and smiled politely. Miss Hallie held her ground, pointing at me.

"Is this your chauffeur's boy? He's grown up since I saw him last, but I thought so. I heard you'd taken an outside boy into your house and were making a great deal of him. They said you're afraid to sleep in the house alone. I don't know why. I stayed alone in my house for years and nobody had to sleep in and look after me."

Miss Alexandria grimaced. Taking her guest's arm, she took her into the library, helped her off with her coat and hat and handed them to Fanny who had appeared at the sound of the bell.

"I see you still have your maids to do your work for you," Miss Hallie said in the grating voice of the deaf. "I told my people over the mountain I didn't know if I wanted to come today or not. They were giving me a birthday dinner over there and all my friends would be at the table. I hated to miss it but I told them I didn't know if I'd ever hear from you again if I turned you down."

Miss Alexandria led her to a big red leather chair and wrote with a pencil on the pad she had ready.

"We're glad you could come."

Miss Hallie read it and pushed it away.

"I told your chauffeur I only hoped I wouldn't catch cold from doing my good deed."

"You used to like winter on the canal," Miss Alexandria wrote.

"That was when Father and Mother were still alive.

Never did I dream I'd ever have to give up our house and go into a private home to live with strangers while you had this big house practically empty and a maid and chauffeur to take care of you and live as you please and nobody in it but yourself. Eighty-four in October, is that right? I thought so, and what you need a whole house to yourself for, I don't know."

Miss Alexandria managed a thin smile and turned to Fanny who appeared at that moment with a tray of highballs which she offered first to Miss Hallie who like a true Morley accepted with alacrity and all was blessedly still for a few moments although, as Miss Alexandria said later, it only added fuel to the fire. There were a glass of ginger ale for me and another highball for Hope who waited until almost the last moment before dinner, then came in, and went up to Miss Hallie, offering her hand.

"Who's this?" the latter demanded of Miss Alexandria who wrote on the pad, "Hope Connor," at which Miss Hallie summarily dropped the hand and stared with disapproval at her cousin.

"Does she stay here with you now, too?"

"Just on a visit," Miss Alexandria wrote.

"I heard she still came around with her mother when she was alive. I said I didn't know whether to believe it or not. I don't understand the things you do, Alix, and you never turn a hair. I wouldn't be able to sleep at night. Thank God we never had anything like that in our family."

"Dinner is ready," Miss Alexandria wrote on the pad and we went out to a beautifully appointed table. Tall white candles burned and flowers bloomed in an enclosed crystal bowl. Miss Hallie bent over them.

"What are they? Artificial? You have them in alcohol? I thought so. You still think real flowers give you hay fever, Alix? Even in the wintertime? Father used to say it was all in your mind. He said people get notions like that in asylums. Here we all were, Morleys like you, and none of us had the belief that pure, innocent and beautiful flowers could make us sick."

Seldom when we were alone did Miss Alexandria have grace said at the table, but now resignedly she indicated Miss Hallie to go ahead and bowed her own head a punctilious inch or two. We all followed suit while the visitor prayed aloud in her strident voice. Fanny stood meekly by with her head down, I'm sure the most devout of us all. Miss Alexandria's upturned eyes kept following her cousin's lips to see when she would be done.

Miss Hallie ate ravenously. She took second helpings of most everything. Dinner seemed interminable to me. I said to myself, thank God, when the birthday cake with one large candle was finally set on the table in front of her while the rest of us sat back and waited for her to cut it. But Miss Hallie was in no hurry. This was her hour and she was going to make the most of it. For a long time she sat there with the candle burning while she told us of

other and happier birthday dinners and what gifts she had
received.

"Don't you want to blow it out and have your wish?"
Miss Alexandria prompted on the pad.

"You always want to rush me, Alix," Miss Hallie told
her. "At our house we never hurried. Of course, we didn't
have maids to get the most out of every minute like you.
I remember how your father rushed my father into selling
Grandfather's land that would now be worth a great deal
of money. I could even have my own house and maid if
I wanted. Father thought everybody was honest like he
was, especially his own brother. The rest of us had to
suffer for it all our lives. I have only one consolation.
What little we had was made honorable and upright. I
told them where I stay I wouldn't want to change places
with you, Alix, for all your money. You know what the
Bible says, the sins of the father are visited on the children.
The mills of God grind slowly but they grind exceedingly
small."

Miss Alexandria started to write on the pad, then tore
the sheet up wearily. Her cousin went on.

"I didn't inherit a fortune like you, Alix, but we could
always tell right from wrong. I don't forget how it used
to upset my mother that your mother would go out buggy
riding alone with your Uncle Asa, just those two out in
the country by themselves and nobody to keep watch on
them, and everybody knowing what kind of a man your

Uncle Asa was. I remember Mother told us girls never to go in his house alone. We always had to have one or two other girls with us. But when my mother spoke to your mother about it, she told her that my mother had an evil mind, that she enjoyed buggy rides with her brother-in-law, that it helped her invalidism and she would keep on taking them as long as she pleased. Father said your father could do nothing about it because he was in the coal business with your Uncle Asa and that's where your money came from."

I watched Miss Alexandria closely but all I saw was the same thin grim smile. If she turned off her hearing aid during her cousin's reproaches or looked elsewhere than her lips, I didn't see it. She seemed bound to stand up under the punishment. It relieved me when the front door sounded and Dr. Howell appeared in the dining room.

"Our doctor," Miss Alexandria wrote on the pad.

"Oh, doctor!" Miss Hallie said, brightening and for a moment I thought I had a glimpse of the beautiful young girl that had been. "I've heard about you. I want to see you and talk to you about my legs before you go." She blew out the candle at once and let Fanny cut the cake.

When my father came with the car, I could see that Miss Hallie didn't want to go. She kept putting it off. In the hall she shook hands with Miss Alexandria but not with Hope or me. In the vestibule she spoke to her cousin confidentially. Back in the library Hope and I could hear every word.

"I shouldn't think you'd let that girl come here as you do, Alix. With everybody knowing who she is and who her mother was and what your own sister did. All she wants is to be in your will and you're a fool if you let her. The boy, too. I'm sure his father put him up to it. He wouldn't have enough sense by himself."

All we could hear from Miss Alexandria was her polite good-byes. She smiled hollowly as she came back to the library, sprawled on a chair and fanned her face with her hand.

"Oh, oh, oh! What one must put up with sometimes! Perhaps now, Hope, you know what I mean."

"I think you did very well, Alexandria. You held yourself in beautifully."

Miss Alexandria sat up.

"Indeed and double, I think I did, child. But then I've had years and years of practice. Really and truly, after that, Eulalie doesn't seem so bad. The poor girl's been angling for an invitation every letter. She never did that in the wintertime before. She always wanted to get away from the Maryland heat. It's cruel of me not to invite her. This house has always had her since she was a small girl and then after she married, Jack was always off on the high seas. We never blamed him. But having Eulalie here in the winter is much too much."

For days she went around with pale resolved face and eyes but in the end wrote as we knew she would sooner or later inviting her cousin to come.

The Aristocrat

"I want to know why she isn't in Sweetwater any more," she excused her bounty. "She never tells. Her postmark was Washington for a while, then it was this place near where the President goes to try to postpone the end of the world. There's something up and it's not good or she would have told me about it."

Chapter x

MISS ALEXANDRIA invited Miss Eulalie for Christmas but it turned out that she was in the hospital. She came later on, for Easter and to stay for the wedding. Hope was getting married in June, not to the stock broker from Baltimore but to the young minister from Philadelphia.

"She'll have a hellish life," Miss Alexandria informed the doctor. "But then she's a Morley and does as she pleases. We'll just have to act like we don't know what she's in for."

Preparations for the wedding were already under way when Miss Eulalie arrived in March looking smaller, shrunken, incredibly quiet and subdued, not quite real. She picked up a little after Easter when excitement over the approaching marriage had begun to color the household.

"They're all coming," Miss Alexandria announced in May. "No one wants to miss it. The Princess Vershaliv accepts with pleasure. The Eugene DuPonts say they are delighted to accept. Blanche's old friend, Marcella, will be here with her charming husband. They've been in Nice for the winter. The Traskers will be here and the Sintons and Cecily Marconis and her family. The only one won't come is Cousin Hallie. But then I knew she wouldn't on account of Hope. I told Hope it was God's blessing. She's having Mother's ruby red wedding dress refitted. It's water taffeta. Mother had it put away with scads of tissue in that black satiny box I showed you one time. Not a break in it. Hope could have put it right on and gone out. Of course, the drop sleeves might look a little strange downtown and she'd have had to hold up the train."

"My mother's was gray," Miss Eulalie said. "All the wedding dresses around Sweetwater were gray or black during wartime. It wasn't till after the war that they started bursting out in bright colors."

"Well, of course," Miss Alexandria told her, "Father was in the Army and they couldn't very well be married before. I guess they could have but Father would have had to miss some battles. I told Hope it would make her look like one of those figures in museums but she wanted it. She wanted a caterer, too, but I said, no. This house has always served its guests and will as long as I live. Polly and old Mary are coming for the kitchen. Mary never says anything fit to print but she gave ten years of her life to me and I'm devoted to her. Oh, oh, oh! what a friend she was to me. Fortunately she has a bad knee and won't be able to leave the kitchen. Carrie's coming to run the stairs. She's one of our girls. Roxie will be upstairs. Everything she is she owes to this house. Really and truly, it will be like old times, hellish and exciting. I can hardly wait."

I couldn't either, not for the wedding but for it to be over. For one thing, I had to give up my room and sleep at home. At the last minute a couch for Miss Eulalie was put in Miss Alexandria's bedroom. The house had been gone over from top to bottom, some thirty rugs vacuumed, the storage in the bedrooms on the third floor taken out to the stable. My father was busy driving to Lancaster and Harrisburg for guests who flew or rode on trains none of which rumbled through Unionville any more. The Rev. Danner called almost daily, beaming, bringing his ecclesiastical presence and leaving his blessing. Since the bridegroom was Lutheran, he would perform the ceremony.

"Aren't you glad Hope is joining your church?" Miss Eulalie said pleased.

"It's not my church," Miss Alexandria told her. "I was dragooned like one of those medieval converts with a gun or sword held over him. I'm not even sure I'm Reformed any more. I can't abide people or institutions who change their names. It's unstable."

Miss Eulalie did not pick up the argument and I was again aware that she was a changed and chastened woman. After a while Miss Alexandria gave up trying to cross swords with her, finding no pleasure in it. Hope and her young minister were married in the bay window of the long Morley parlor as Miss Blanche had been before her. All through the ceremony I could see Miss Alexandria cast disapproving looks at her cousin crying silently into her handkerchief. The latter went through the festivities afterward almost mutely, passing up chances to pour into fresh ears her memories of Jack, the fine doorways of Portsmouth and her grandfather's thousand-acre plantation along the Potomac.

Miss Alexandria was plainly baffled. However, not until the Princess Vershaliv and the Eugene DuPonts had left along with the Traskers, Sintons and Cecily Marconis, and after Polly, Carrie, old Mary and Roxie had departed from under the back stairs did the truth come out. At the first meal by ourselves, Miss Alexandria fixed an eye on her cousin.

"I've known you for eighty years, Eulalie, but I never saw you like this. You're either senile or dying with cirrhosis of the liver. Now I want you to tell me which, so Dr. Howell can start working on you."

Miss Eulalie gave little smothered sounds of disavowal. She protested there was nothing, which only put iron into Miss Alexandria's soul.

"I bet a cow it has something to do with your namesake."

Miss Eulalie cried out in sudden pain but Miss Alexandria had held back too long to give up now. Knowing she had touched a tender spot, she went on probing pitilessly until little by little it all came out that the fine new house Eulalie Smith had built in Washington had looked bare as a church until Miss Eulalie helped furnish it with a few of her things which she didn't need and which her namesake would get in the end anyhow.

"Not the Afghanistan in your parlor that you promised me?" Miss Alexandria asked.

Miss Eulalie flinched and mumbled something how Eulalie Smith had loved it and how nothing else could have dressed up the big Washington house living room so beautifully as that rug.

"I loved it, too," Miss Alexandria said grimly. "You didn't give her the two Bokharas Jack brought from Beirut that you swore would be mine some day."

Miss Eulalie said nothing, only bowed her head. She did it so meekly and submissively I hoped Miss Alexandria would stop now and show mercy. But in my heart I knew better. I remembered her story of how her father, the Captain, driving home from a G A R encampment in the Hegins Valley had overtaken Sergeant Zimmerman seventy years old on the Broad Mountain. The Sergeant was on foot with ten or twelve miles still to tramp, the Captain alone in his buggy with his two famous spanking sorrels. But they had been sworn enemies in the regiment and the Captain never stopped. And now Miss Alexandria never stopped for her cousin.

"I hope to God you still have that magnificent inlaid

mother-of-pearl jewel box that was to be Hope's? The one Jack brought from Yokohama with the Satsuma vase?" she accused and went on mercilessly to the brass ship's lantern from the *Kearsarge,* the set of Wedgwood in the Phoebe pattern made before the bombing of Coventry destroyed the molds, and the blue and white cups that George Washington had drank out of at the plantation.

It turned out in the end that everything had been given and the house sensibly turned into cash to pay off Eulalie Smith's mortgage so Miss Eulalie could spend the rest of her days in Washington with Eulalie Smith and her two daughters one of whom was named Eulalie also.

"I couldn't live alone in the Sweetwater house any more, Alix," she defended herself. "She was going to get it in the will anyhow but then the inheritance taxes would have eaten it up because she's not my daughter, unfortunately, and you know how much the government takes out and this way there was no inheritance tax and it would have worked out fine, Alix, if Eulalie hadn't got sick and if I hadn't been too old and feeble to do the house work, and Edgar had to put me in a nursing home. You couldn't expect him to take care of me and the house and the children too. He had to go to the office every day. It was a beautiful nursing home, too, Alix, but then it cost too much and they had to take me to another one out of Washington where it wouldn't be so horribly expensive."

I never saw Miss Alexandria so angry before or since. "I'm not surprised," she said, although it was plain she was. "The Fortunes never could hold on to anything. Your mother had to keep Uncle Sam's money in her own name or somebody would have flimflammed him out of it. Thank the Lord you still have your trust fund. I hope you changed your will so she doesn't get hold of that."

Miss Eulalie winced.

"Who else could I think of to give it to, Alix?" she asked pathetically. "You have all you'll ever need."

Miss Alexandria looked speechless.

"I knew it," she said, savagely attacking her apple pie. "You lick the hand that beats you."

Miss Eulalie wiped her eyes.

"The Bible says, though the Lord slay me I will love him."

"But it doesn't say Eulalie Smith. I don't think you love her at all, Eulalie, only her name. If you really and truly did, you wouldn't let her get away with such a performance. What do you think her conscience is going to do to her when she's old and about to die and knows she stripped you of everything and then turned you out? What's she going to say to St. Peter? You could very well have kept her out of heaven."

One thing I have learned in my short life is that a quick temper often covers a soft underbelly. Miss Alexandria continued to explode from time to time with what she thought of Miss Eulalie and her namesake. Perhaps it was a good thing she did. There inevitably followed a counterbalance of Morley hospitality, breakfasts in bed, drives through the countryside, companionship in the evening and the services of Dr. Howell whenever her cousin wanted them. The doctor groaned, my father and Fanny murmured but Miss Alexandria continued to sail on, repairing her failing sympathies from time to time with fresh outbreaks on the two Eulalies.

How it might have ended, I have no idea, but during a mild spell in November, the town dump caught fire. A surface fire would have been easy enough to put out. This was a slow burn of everything that had been buried deep under the cover of soil that Miss Alexandria had the town put down, layer upon layer until at places it was twelve feet thick. The fall had been dry and the conflagration spread below until smoke poured up from a dozen widely separated places. By day it rose into the firmament. At night it collected and drifted slowly into town with its choking stench of smoldering garbage, cardboard and old tires.

The second day Miss Alexandria failed to come home for supper. Old Mary lay seriously ill and Fanny thought she might have gone to see her. She had me run out to Chickentown but no one had seen her there. Not until two o'clock in the morning did she appear through the front door. She looked ghastly.

"Well, we did it. It's out!" she announced triumphantly.

"Alix. What have you been doing all this time? Where in God's name have you been?" Miss Eulalie demanded.

"I've been to the dump," Miss Alexandria said as she

might have said to war or the colliery or the Army-Navy game on Franklin Field.

"Whew! You don't need to tell me. I can smell it on you. Now you'll have to burn all your clothes."

"I must take you down some time, Eulalie," Miss Alexandria told her. "Every citizen should be made to smell his dump for an hour at close range. He wouldn't believe modern civilization could permit such a vile, foul, rotten and loathsome hole in its midst. At first I couldn't breathe. I don't see how Jakey stands it."

"But why in the world did you of all people have to go there? Why didn't you make the town council do it?"

Miss Alexandria gave a hollow laugh.

"That's rich. I saw one councilman all night, and the mayor not at all. They have the honor. They don't need to work at it. If it hadn't been for their faithful bulldozer driver, the whole town would have suffocated. I knew Jakey's father and grandfather but I never knew the boy before. I told his wife when she brought his midnight supper, I hoped she appreciated a man you could depend on. He set up a gasoline engine on the riverbank and pumped water till everything was a sea of mud. I'm wet to my knees and I'm sure he must have been soaked all over."

"You're crazy going to a place like that. What could you do?"

"I could hold the fort with Jakey and keep him company. We talked politics and philosophy and a little history. I told him about Vesuvius and Mt. Etna. Now

I'm going to bed. I must go down first thing in the morning to see it doesn't start up again."

She never got there. During the night she rang for Fanny who called Dr. Howell. I heard nothing of it until breakfast. Fanny told me then what the doctor had said. Miss Alexandria was completely exhausted and had caught cold in the bargain. It had brought on an asthma and heart attack that had almost killed her. From now on, dump or no dump, she would have to stay in bed. I went in to see her after getting home from school. She looked ashen, lifeless, hardly visible under the covers. Only her eyes, when she opened them, had the inexpressible look they always had without her glasses, a sage look as if this was no world of her own making but she'd put it through its paces.

Next day she grew worse. Dr. Howell ordered a night nurse and said he'd get others as soon as Miss Alexandria let him. Fanny at last could go to her own room to sleep. My father was plainly worried. He stayed around the house most of the day doing odd jobs. In the evening he sat on his red-cushioned barroom chair by the furnace. But Miss Eulalie flourished. Suddenly she was the well and fortunate one. Bent, ancient, little more than Kipling's rag and bone and a hank of hair, she kept scurrying tirelessly around the house, talking as of old, driving me and the rest of us almost mad. All the while Miss Alexandria continued to sink. She would take nothing now but tea. I think we all expected her to pass on over the weekend but it was the unsurprising Miss Eulalie who surprised us. Fanny found her, a strangely silent, weightless, crumpled-up ball in her bed when she went in with her breakfast in the morning.

The doctor who came at once ordered us not to breathe a word to Miss Alexandria but he might have saved his breath. She had known Fanny's face for too many years not to read something new written on it now.

"What's happened in this house?" she demanded, and when Fanny stammered there was nothing, she sat up abruptly in bed and ordered her to tell all or suffer for it. Instead of crushing Miss Alexandria, the news acted like a shot in the arm. She got out of bed, defying Fanny, my father and the doctor when he came.

"Who do you suppose is going to bury her if I don't?" was all she would say. She had us call Ben Stetler the undertaker. "Now all I want you to do, Benny," she told him when he came, "is fix her up a little so she won't fall apart on the way and take her to Sweetwater. She's outlived two undertakers down there but the third is supposed to know what she wants. She's told a woman exactly how her hair's to be done. All her friends are in Sweetwater and you can tell the undertaker to make the announcement when they can come. She always said she wanted the service in her own house, but she has no house any more to have it in."

"Should I call Mrs. Smith?" Fanny asked meekly when the body was gone.

Miss Alexandria didn't answer. Her face looked cruel. Only the next evening did she let Fanny telephone her, staying in bed herself until the morning of the funeral. Then she got up very early and my father drove her to Sweetwater for the service and after that to the dinner she had ordered at the Sweetwater House for everyone who attended. I had to go along. Since it was Sunday, Dr. Howell elected to ride with us, "to try to keep the second corpse alive," he told my father. But he had no need to. She went through everything like an iron woman, shaking hands and exchanging a few words with all of Miss Eulalie's friends, recalling those from Sweetwater, including Eulalie Smith herself although I saw Miss Alexandria's mouth contract until it was little more than an icy smirk. Afterward she took refuge in the company of Hope and her clergyman husband who had driven down from Philadelphia. They accompanied us and the hearse to Arlington where Hope's husband said fitting words over the grave.

Looking back several times from the front seat where I sat with my father on the way home, I found Miss Alexandria sunken in her corner of the back seat, holding on grimly with one hand to the strap. Most of the ride she stayed that way, mute, deathlike, as if it were too much of an effort to speak but more than once I thought I saw her lips move and wondered if she were repeating to herself some of the bitter things she had wanted to say to Eulalie Smith and hadn't.

Chapter xi

From that time on we knew it was just a matter of time. My father said that Miss Eulalie's death had done something to her. Miss Alexandria seldom mentioned it. Her only reference was something spoken to me a few days after the funeral. She was sitting up in bed playing solitaire.

"I think I'll tell the Lord, Tommy, He ought to let me in no matter how many wrong things I did. I mean because of all the people I buried. I don't count Mother and Father and Blanche, and Hope when they shipped her back. That was my business. Or the times I took cups and saucers and silver to one of the cousins to help feed the mourners. I mean those I had to bury myself. There was Bess Stokely. She didn't even have a preacher. I said to Benny Stetler who can we get? He said Rev. Youse would do it. I said I don't even know the man and he doesn't know me. 'Yes, he does,' he said, 'but even if he didn't, I think he'd do it,' and he did. It was January and hellish cold. We all nearly froze on the cemetery. We had twenty people staying at the house and the first thing I did on coming back was give them all shots of whisky."

She played a red nine on a black ten.

"Arnold, her husband, was next. It was July and hot as Hades. I don't know if you can draw any conclusions from that but I can. I never could abide him."

She started to leaf by threes through the rest of the cards in her hand.

"There were more after that I won't go into. Two lived away from Unionville all their lives but they wanted to come back here to be buried. I don't know why. Or maybe I do. But I don't know why I had to do it for them. Then after all those, didn't I have to bury Wayne Huning! He died upstate somewhere. He always said he wanted everybody to have a highball at his funeral. But his house was closed and Cousin Amy's house was closed and there was no place but here. She never would let whisky in her house anyhow. She used to pour perfectly good Scotch down the drain. It made Cousin Harry wild. He couldn't look at it. I told Lee Parry, here's the stuff. You do what Wayne wanted. Then I went upstairs and took off my hearing aid. I heard a little afterward what happened. Dr. Heller, who sewed me up, told me he'd never been to such a funeral. I didn't ask the particulars but I had an idea."

She went back to her game, playing what cards she had left, but it was no go.

"And then," she went on, "Ellen Jennings said to me, 'Alix, you buried all these other people. I wish you'd do it for me when the time comes.' She was head nurse so long at the Friends Hospital in Philadelphia, I figured she ought to know enough to outlive me. But she didn't and they shipped her up here to me. Well, that was the limit! But I did what she wanted."

She messed up the cards with both hands preparatory to shuffling again.

"And now here I am with no one to bury me. But I won't know it fortunately. I think it quite clever of the Lord to arrange it that way. It's hard enough on the living. What if the dead had to go through it, too?"

Of late, I could see that she was getting her things in order, burning letters and photographs. One day she told me about her father's youngest brother. She just called him Jim.

"I was sitting here last night, Tommy, and wanted to know something. I mean something that happened a long time ago. I went over in my mind who could tell me and, by jingoes, there wasn't anybody. I was the last. It gave me a start. I thought I better ask if there's anything you want to know while I'm still here. Say, about your Grandfather Jim. Good Lord! he was your great grandfather. No, that can't be true. Why, I never heard of such a thing! But I guess it must be so. What do you know about him?"

"I know he went through the Civil War," I said.

"A lot of trash went through the Civil War," she told

me, taking me down. "My father always said so and that his brother, Jim, was one. You know, there's bad blood in every family and when it comes out you have a black sheep. It skipped my generation and it skipped yours, but it came out in your great grandfather. He wasn't queer, just peculiar. Among other things he used to wear a big ridiculous Western hat and strike poses like one of Frederic Remington's cowboys. The boys knew he carried a watch in every pocket so they'd ask him the time. They wanted to see him bring them out one after the other. He claimed he took them from dead rebels who didn't need them anyhow. Father didn't like that but he never said too much till Jim got a girl not much older than I in trouble and took her to live with him in his place on Back Street. Her name was Molly Clump and she was your great-grandmother. From that time on Father forbade him to come to the house. Jim always worshipped Mother and about that time one of our maids got sick and the other left saying she wasn't going to do all the work in this big place herself. We had house guests and Blanche and I were in the kitchen trying to get dinner when there was a knock on the back door and there was Molly. 'I heard you were in trouble and came to offer myself,' she said. We told Mother and she said to take her in and be thankful. She made Father let her stay when he came home from the colliery, but Father said that didn't go for Jim. A good many times when Father was out, Jim would come to the back door. "Molly, do you think Lolly would see me?'

he'd say and Molly would say, 'Well, Jim, I don't know if she will or won't but she can't do more than say no.' Then she'd go upstairs. 'Mrs. Morley, you may get cross at me for this but Jim's down and says he'd give anything to see you.' 'You can bring him up, Molly,' Mother would say. She always saw Jim and listened to his hard-luck stories but she sent him home before Father came from the colliery."

Miss Alexandria must have seen the crestfallen look on my face.

"Now you mustn't be ashamed of your great-grand-mother. She was a good cook and housekeeper and legally married like anybody else. Grandmother Morley saw to that. In school Molly always called me Alexandria but when she came in service to us, I told her she'd have to call me Miss Alexandria or nothing at all. She did. When she left, she thanked us and said we never hurt her feelings and she would think kindly of us, especially Mother."

That winter Miss Alexandria had grown incredibly thin. She said it was physically impossible to sit on a hard chair any more.

"Indeed and double, child," she told me, "I never knew I dragged around such hellish bones."

Her hands troubled me, fragile, pale, raised with thick dark veins, the emaciated fingers heavy with jeweled rings. They seemed incongruous, medieval, almost from the grave. The worst was their trembling. When she raised a shaking glass, I watched hypnotized to see if it reached her lips without spilling. It always did but the effort must have been prodigious. If it bothered her, she made no comment.

She did say one or two things around the holidays.

"Is it really Christmas?" she asked me. "It doesn't seem like Christmas."

"I guess you had wonderful Christmases when you were young," I said.

She gave one of her sardonic laughs.

"Christmas was hellish." She remained silent a while. "Mother always gave around two hundred presents. She'd make out her list and Blanche and I had to go to Philadelphia and do her buying. For two or three days we shopped like mad. Maybe she'd have down just "a scarf" or "stockings" or "gloves." If she couldn't think of anything, she'd write, "for two or three dollars" and we'd have to find something. We bought scarves and gloves and stockings by the dozen."

"How'd you know the size?"

"We didn't. Mother was never bothered by details. We'd have to guess. Gloves were always five and a half or six and those with bigger hands had to squeeze in. Stockings were number nine. Then we had to write notes for each one and say they were from Mother."

"Couldn't she write any herself?"

"She could but she didn't. She never did anything. She was a born invalid. I don't know anybody who could get more out of you with a smile. One time we had to buy handbags all alike. Most times it was material for dresses. Half the people in this town had their dress goods selected by Blanche and me once upon a time. We heard after Christmas people would go to each other's houses to see what their friends got from Mother."

"She must have done something," I stammered.

"She didn't need to. Father adored her. Uncle Asa adored her. We all did, at least most of the time. She only had to look at you and you'd do anything for her. Every morning she had me wash her face and then go down and order her breakfast. First thing she did was drink a small pitcher of cream. She claimed it saved her life and let her live to be eighty-six."

Miss Alexandria peered out trying to see the snow on the spruces.

"One Christmas she got it into her head she was going to give sewing tables to a dozen friends. Somebody had given her one years before. It opened and closed. We got Mr. Goebel to make them. He grumbled and grumbled. We had to varnish them ourselves. The whole house smelled of varnish. Then we had to cut silk pockets on each side and sew them with gold tape. Fanny still has one of those tables she got hold of and thinks the world of it. But they were a hellish nightmare to us. And all the while Mother sat there sweet and patient. She stayed that way through everything."

I kept silent. Miss Alexandria threw me a glance.

"All this time she gave no Christmas presents in the

house except to the servants. When I was fifteen or six-teen I told her I'd like a Christmas present myself. 'What do you want?' she asked. 'A diamond ring,' I said. 'No daughter of mine can wear a diamond ring till she's eight-een,' she said. 'Hallie has one,' I told her. 'Let others do as they wish,' she said. 'I won't.' When I went to Mrs. Somers' school, I wrote home that my roommate had night dresses and underthings with lace and ribbons and I felt like a nun in a nunnery. But Mother wouldn't change and when I got older I realized it was all cheap trumpery bought by people who were nobody and mine was nain-sook imported from England and every inch cut and measured and sewed in this house. That was Mother. When I was twenty-one, Father bought me the ring I wanted with a diamond and sapphires. 'You take off that ring,' Mother said when she saw it. 'Only a fast woman would wear anything like that.' But Father and I worked on her and she gave in."

It was late. The bell of the Lutheran church across the street began to ring for the midnight service. Miss Alex-andria, who had her hearing aid on, asked what it was. She made a face against the sound until it stopped.

"Yes, we were all played out till Christmas was over. All of us except Mother. She loved it. The night before Christmas we had to trim the tree. Then we had highballs. After that we young people played poker till morning. All my life I was expected to gamble with Richard and Archie and their friends so they wouldn't go play in some hay mow and burn the barn down as happened a couple of times. The whole gang came to Christmas dinner. It lasted hours. We had everything from oysters down. Mother should have stayed in the South. She was used to being waited on by darkies. But don't think she didn't know what was going on. Her nurse the last year of her life told me that at night when all was quiet in the house, she'd call her in and put her finger on her lips. That meant you must never breathe a word of what I tell you. The nurse would cross her heart and Mother would tell her the secrets of the town. How she found out some of them we never knew."

There was the sound of voices on the street, people going to church. After a while I could hear singing. The voices were louder and more joyous when they came out. "Merry Christmas. Merry Christmas!" they called. Miss Alexandria asked me what it was. She didn't make a face now. When all was silent again, I thought she listened for more voices and there weren't any. She sat silent now a long time.

"Is it as deadly in here as it seems, Tommy?" she asked. "Jennie Schuyler once told me that when you get old, your friends don't come to see you any more. I didn't believe her. I thought it was the Schuylers they didn't want to come and see. I still do."

She sat there and it was hard to tell what she was thinking. I knew the Schuylers were gone now. So was the Rev. Danner. He had a big church, they said, in Lancaster. Miss Alexandria didn't speak of him any more.

"My friends all died," she told me. "I hold them responsible for my loneliness." She laughed grudgingly. "I still can't believe it's me, Tommy, sitting alone in this house day after day. It just shows what you can do when you have to. You know, Bessie has her beauty shop in Uncle Asa's house. In an apartment. I used to go in and have my hair done. She asked me the first time how I liked it. She meant her shop. I hadn't dared think about it or I'd have sat down and cried. Here I'd have been sitting in one of Uncle Asa's big chairs. Over there would be Cousin Lucy's grand piano. Aunt Ruby would come in from the conservatory and ask if I'd stay for dinner. Uncle Asa would be in the library reading his New York paper and smoking one of the cigars he had made for him in Havana. But I didn't tell her that. I said her shop looked very nice. I was brought up to be polite even if it killed you."

She took off her glasses and held them up to squint through.

"I don't need to be polite to you, Tommy. You're family. I can tell you I disliked your great Aunt Lou intensely. She'd come up every summer and stay with us for months and criticize us young folks. When she had letters ready to mail, I'd disappear so I wouldn't have to carry them to the post office. She must have been ninety the last summer she spent here. In the fall Father made arrangements to take her back to her house in Philadelphia. I was at the piano when she came in the parlor and sat on the bench beside me. 'I want to thank you for all you've done for me this summer,' she said. 'You'll never know how much it meant to a lonely old woman.' "

Miss Alexandria gazed at me as if to say, now don't get any wrong ideas, Master Thomas. I'm just warning you for yourself someday. You think it can't happen to you.

She was only a shadow of herself these days.

"When I look in the glass, I cry bloody murder," she once told me.

Just the same she met inflexibly her few remaining social obligations. The doctor had to keep coming to Sunday dinner for which she dressed painstakingly. Seeing her descending the stairs, holding to the banister with one hand, gowned, her hair faultlessly brushed and put up by Fanny, a string of real pearls around her corded throat, her face drained of blood and scornful of rouge or lipstick, the familiar diamonds glittering on her fingers, I would think of lines quoted by my English teacher at school.

> Why so large a cost, having so short a lease,
> Dost thou on thy fading mansion spend?

That sonnet had been written three hundred years before by a poet of whom Miss Alexandria had a complete set but, I'm sure, never read. At least she never quoted him. Those she did quote were her contemporaries, her

mother and father, certain of her maids, Eulalie, the
Princess Vershaliv, the Eugene DuPonts, Blanche, Jack
Ferguson, Richard, Mrs. Somers of Mrs. Somers' school,
Aunt Sudy, Aunt Phi and Uncle Sam. Mostly she made
her own quotes. Almost every evening in the library she
talked to me over her table of solitaire. She still never went
to bed before midnight, claimed she wouldn't sleep if she
did. It was the Morley blood, she said, accustomed to
staying up all night.

"We're not like the Schuylers," she added. "They
marched upstairs every evening at ten sharp. Even the
bridge game had to stop."

When finally she had to take to her bed, she took it as
an indignity unworthily put upon her by fate. When I
came into the bedroom, she almost ignored me, as if by
seeing her there I contributed to her humiliation. She
would lie with her eyes closed but I knew by her moving
hands that she wasn't asleep. She didn't want to talk now.
One night she got out of bed by herself and fell. After that
one or the other of us had to be with her at all times. Finally the doctor got her a hospital bed with sides like a
crib so she couldn't get out alone. She lay in it like an
animal in a cage, her eyes burning through the bars. My
father said she wasn't Miss Alexandria any more. It troubled me. I had heard of old people who got queer, weren't
themselves, but I never believed it could happen to Miss
Alexandria.

Then one afternoon I came home from school and

learned that the long-looked-for had finally happened. I didn't know whether to feel sad or relieved.

My father met me in the front hall. He looked hard.

"She deserved to go more peaceful," he told me.

"Was she scared?"

"Morleys never scare. Her father went back to war when he didn't have to. So did Mr. Jim. I never saw Miss Alexandria scared. She wouldn't run from the devil himself."

Benny Stetler came down the stairs at that moment and my father went out with him. I sought Fanny in the kitchen. She was standing mutely in the middle of the room, her face grave and cruel. It was as if the world had come to an end.

"What happened, Fanny?" I wanted to know. "Did she suffer?"

"No, no. I'm sure not," she said, but she wouldn't meet my eyes. "I never looked for it today. I'm glad the minister was with her." She didn't say whether it was the Lutheran or Reformed.

"I hope he knew not to pray out loud for her."

"He knew." Fanny still wouldn't look at me. "I heard Miss Alexandria tell him a couple of weeks ago. But he stayed too long. She got tired. If he hadn't been the minister, I'd have told him to go. She turned white. I think he thought she was dying and that's what started him praying for her."

"Not out loud, Fanny!"

"I thought his praying might make her better," Fanny said earnestly. "He knows all the nice prayer words. I could see Miss Alexandria reading his lips. But when she started to talk to him, I knew she wasn't herself. You know how some sick people get. She thought he was somebody else. I apologized to him afterward."

"Who did she think he was?"

"She took him for the steward at the Chamber City country club. She ordered him to make two highballs, one for her and one for me. I felt sorry for him. He kept telling her he was the minister but she wouldn't have it. You know how she could get. 'I know you perfectly well,' she told him. 'You are William. I hired and trained you myself. Now will you please go to the pantry and mix those highballs. You know how I like them. And don't come back without them.' I felt terrible for him. He just stood there and got red and didn't know what to do. Miss Alexandria kept staring at him. I never saw her look so hard at anybody. When he didn't go, she started to get out of bed but she couldn't. Then she laid back on her pillows white as death and closed her eyes. When I got Dr. Howell, she was gone. I felt so bad for the minister, I tried to explain she was delirious, out of her mind."

I looked at Fanny and she looked away. We both knew Miss Alexandria wasn't delirious. I remembered what she had often said, that if anybody ever prayed out loud for her when she was sick, she'd run him out of the house. She hadn't been able to do that but she had done the next best thing, a grimly humorous thing, macabre, exactly like her. That night when I went to bed I didn't feel too badly about her going any more. She hadn't broken at the end. She was still her old self.

For months, things that Miss Alexandria had said when she was alive kept coming back to me. What I remembered most was something told me when she was still up and about.

"When I die, Tommy," she had said, "there won't be anybody around here like me any more. I'm not in business. I'm beholden to nobody. I speak my mind and do as I please. I'm the last, and when I'm gone, that will be the end."

ADDENDA

Miss Alexandria
on Her Mother

MOTHER never liked children until they grew up. "Go away," she would say to me. "Do something else." Aunt Sudy used to chide her for it. Sometimes when they played cards there would be a loud thump in the house. "What's that?" Aunt Sudy would want to know. "It's nothing," Mother would tell her, "just the baby falling off the nurse's lap." My nurse would rock me in a chair and we'd both fall asleep.

❧❦❧

It wasn't that Mother wasn't kind. She simply had no use for children. Once I complained that my leg hurt. "Don't pay attention to her," Mother said. "She imagines it." "I want to see, Lolly," Aunt Sudy said. She got down on the floor with me. She found a needle in my leg and

139

pulled it out with her teeth. "It would have come out anyway," Mother said. "It always does."

❖❰◇❰❰

Mother never liked family dinners. They were too stiff and tiresome. She knew in advance what every one would say. "Mix stiff drinks, girls," she told us. "See if you can't stir them up a little."

❖❰◇❰❰

When Father proposed to Mother, she told him she wouldn't raise any children without a nursemaid. She couldn't possibly look after them herself. Father told her she wouldn't have to and she never did.

❖❰◇❰❰

One thing Mother abhorred was a lady smoking. She said to me in her room, "You don't smoke, Alexandria?" "Why, yes I do," I told her. "I think it's degrading. Blanche doesn't." "Of course she does," I told her. She called for Blanche and Blanche admitted it. "Well, I don't want either of you ever to smoke in my presence. If you must be vulgar, do it where I can't see you." Now Father was different. He would order a pack of cigarettes for us with dessert at a hotel, then ask if smoking by ladies was permitted. "Well, it isn't done here," the waiter would generally tell him. "What kind of a hostelry is this?" Father would say.

❖《❖《

One time we hired a new maid from the country. She saw Mother in one of her asthma attacks and was very sympathetic. "Your mother ought to be in a cow stable," she told us. She meant the smell of manure was good for asthma. We never let Mother hear the last of that.

❖《❖《

Mother didn't know how to show affection. She was very practical. We took her to Old Faithful Inn in the Yellowstone. This was in the stagecoach days. She said she would stay in the hotel and watch the geyser from her room. Blanche and I went out to tour the park. At dinner that evening Mother said, "What do they do with people who die here? How do they get them out?" Blanche and I took the hint and got her out the next morning.

❖《❖《

I get my intolerance for crudeness from my mother. She was from the South. When she first came here as a bride she couldn't take Pennsylvania manners. Down in the Maryland countryside she spoke to everybody and everybody spoke to her, especially the old-time darkies who could shame a white person with politeness. The first time she went on a drive up here, she said good morning to a farmer. "Hunh?" he grunted to her. He didn't know her. Why should he speak to her? It was the same when she spoke in town to people she didn't know. They looked at her as if she were queer.

⊰⫟⊱

But like me, Mother never gave up. She fought bad manners all her life. One evening the maid was out and Father and I were playing chess in the library. The bell rang and Mother went to the door. A man from the country stood there. "Say, is the old man in?" he asked. Mother looked at him. Oh, oh, oh, how she could look at you! "You may come in," she said. "Now take off your hat." The frightened man did so. "Don't you know it's impolite to speak to a lady with your hat on, all the more so in a lady's house." "I'm just a farmer from Chonestown, I don't know about such things," he said. "Well, now you know," Mother told him. "Where did you say you were from?" "Near Chonestown," he said. "You must say Jonestown," she told him. "Now say it right, Jonestown." She had him practice. "Now you can go in and see Mr. Morley. He's in the library."

But Mother gave up on some of our maids. They

resisted English like the Welsh. We drank "oranch chuice" most of our lives.

❖❰❖❰❖

Mother never said Captain Morley like other people. It was always Mr. Morley. I think Father had been on the wrong side in the war. If he'd been on General Lee's staff she might have called him Colonel.

❖❰❖❰❖

About once a year in the summertime Mother had the notion she wanted to pick raspberries. It usually happened when Blanche and I were all set to go somewhere. First we had to help her put on an old dress, hat and lace gloves, then carry out her chair, cushions, smelling salts and a little quart kettle. After that one of us would stand and hold an umbrella over her while she picked. Her kettle never had much more than the bottom covered. Blanche and I would have to fill it. Later on she'd enrage us by saying to the first caller, "I picked some raspberries today. It would please me if you would take them along."

❖❰❖❰❖

Like me, Mother had trouble sleeping at night. If she heard something when Father was out, she'd go downstairs with her little brown shawl around her shoulder, holding a candle. One time she found Ray Diehl, a neighbor boy, in the library. He wanted to look up something he heard was racy in one of our books. He said he was never so mortified in his life. There Mrs. Morley stood only in her nightgown but that didn't stop her from acting like she were fully dressed. Mother had heard him pull down the prism lamp from the ceiling.

On Her Father

Y ou know, Father was to go to Russia. He was to be on the crew that built the trans-Siberian Railway. It was a great disappointment when he had to stay home and go in the coal business. He never stopped talking about it.

❖❀❖

Father had a pair of Remington sorrels. They had the same mother and were only a year and a half apart. Mr. Potts in Chamber City offered Father a thousand dollars for the pair. Two days after Father refused, Skip broke his leg in a rotten bridge plank and had to be shot. Scamp grieved so badly, Father had to give him to our farmer to keep. His boy hitched him up with a mule and drove him on the railroad where he was killed. Father was furious. They used to whinny whenever they heard Father's step. He would let me drive the pair and then hide himself on the back seat so people would think a child was driving them alone. Their only fault was like all sorrels, they'd stop once in a while and wouldn't go till they wanted to. It made Father fit to be tied.

❖‹‹❖‹‹

Father wasn't very religious. Once Mother entertained a church delegate overnight in the house. He was here for some synod or other. Father had just brought home a new suit of clothes from his tailor in Philadelphia and laid the box in the bottom drawer of the dresser. It was in the room Mother put the delegate in. When the delegate left, we looked everywhere for Father's suit but never did find it.

❖‹‹❖‹‹

Father always came out in the kitchen to see if the new maid saved string. "If she does that," he'd say, "she'll save more important things." Mother would tip the new girls off. "Now if you don't save string and Mr. Morley sees you, out you go."

On Maids

W HEN A MAID leaves my house, I pride myself that she could serve anywhere. I always said if I lost my money, the only way I could earn a living was to be a maid. But I'd be a perfect one. Or else I'd start an agency and school for maids in New York. Indeed and double, child, training maids was all I ever did. To break them into serving at the table, we'd take turns being the lady. First, she'd sit at my place while I came from the pantry and served her. After that I'd sit there and she'd have to serve me.

＊《＊《

You've no idea of the raw material we sometimes had to work with. Often they were girls out of the field or cow stable. One of them put a silver coffeepot on the stove to boil. One was so homesick for her baby sister out

147

on the farm, she took the statue of Venus de Milo down from the mantel and rocked it in her lap. A girl from the Blue Mountains threw a chicken at Mother who was very particular. "You can clean it yourself!" she yelled. "You may go upstairs and get your things," Mother said. "When you come down, your money will be ready for you." A Herring girl refused to use the back door. "I'm as good as you are," she said. Mother was very patient with her. Her father had told Father he sent her in because they couldn't do anything with her at home, but Father told Mother the girl's mother sent her to learn some of the social graces from Mrs. Morley. Mother had a big flowery hat like the ladies wore those days. One time we were in the library when we saw that hat pass the front window majestically. When the girl came back, Mother gave her a second-best hat for her own. It was still more outrageously flowered than the other.

⊷⊱⊰⊷

The trouble was that most of our girls got married. After that, their husbands wouldn't let them work out or they had babies. Phrany Moyer told Mother that she raised all her children according to what she learned in this house. Her husband became well-to-do. He was invited to bring his wife to a convention at the Buckhill Falls hotel but was scared to eat with all the city people at his

148

table. "Just watch what I do and you'll be all right," Phrany told him. She'd learned the right forks and spoons in this house.

❖❮❖❮

They weren't all dumb by any means. Mother had her hair put up in some new way at Bonds in Philadelphia. That night when she came home she asked Sade to take it down and take notice how she did it. Next morning Sade put it up exactly as they had in the city. Sade was only a maid and laundress but she was sharp as a tack.

❖❮❖❮

"Do you know you are harboring a bad woman in this house?" Aunt Lou once said to Mother. "Yes, I know perfectly and she suits us very well," Mother told her. They meant good old Mary who had I don't know how many children out of wedlock and could swear like a trooper.

❖❮❖❮

I think I told you before about Mary. I adored her. She was afraid of neither man nor devil. She'd take after either one with the butcher knife. Mary had no morals but was an excellent cook. Whenever I made cocktails for my company, I'd have to make two for her, one old fashioned before she served and one afterward. She was very extravagant. I said to her once, "We have to buy so much butter, Mary." You like things to taste good, don't you?" she came back at me. We never knew how much of our butter went home.

⋪⋘⋫⋙

Yes, I know about some servants taking things. They feel they have the right, that it's part of their wages. I told Mr. January it's the fine point in the contract that nobody reads but everybody knows is there. For forty years Sade Kehler worked part time for us and did our washing. She always came up the alley for firewood to start her fire. "Look out there," one of the maids would tell me. "She's got her apron full of your wood again." "Yes, I know," I would say. I don't think she ever started a fire in her life except with wood from our cellar. For years when she worked here she bought our meat from the butcher wagon and I often wondered why we never had the little end part of our lamb roast when it came to the table. You know, that's the best part. Then Mary came into service and went along out to the butcher wagon. Sade bought the roast like usual. "Now cut off the little end piece," she said. "No, you don't," Mary told him. "That goes with it." We had wondered all those years where it went.

✣❊✣❊

Not only the lamb roast. Whenever Sade needed anything, she would come and help herself. Every night we'd hear the refrigerator door open and close. What's she taking now, we would say upstairs. We didn't mind too much. It was expected, quite legitimate and didn't cost too much. Why, those days you could buy a dozen spring chickens for a dollar and a half and I don't know how many shad.

✣❊✣❊

It was harder on Horace. He was Sade's husband. He told somebody when Sade put something special on the table, he always wondered if it came from the Morley house. He hadn't dared ask so he'd tell himself, well, if it did, they must have sent it over for me. Then he could eat it with good grace.

✣❊✣❊

Yes, I know all about servants from Grandfather's house in Maryland. Old Aunt Phi died in one of Aunt

Sudy's nightgowns between a pair of Aunt Sudy's sheets with her head on one of Aunt Sudy's pillow cases and a handkerchief embroidered S.F. in her hand.

❖❖❖

Now Fanny is nothing like that. She's given twenty-seven years of her life to me. After the first ten years, Mike said he needed her at home. He was in the green goods business. "Now don't worry, Miss Alexandria," she said. "I'll bring my daughter-in-law down and show her what to do and you'll never know I'm gone." She did just that and we had both Polly and her for a week. Then Fanny left and things ran just as smooth as before. I could hardly tell the difference.

❖❖❖

Sade Kehler could tell a good story. She loved to come in and tell them to Mother. Mother would see the expression on her face and say, "Now, Sade, if you have anything interesting to say about anyone, I'll be glad to hear it. But I don't want to hear scandal." Well, something juicy would happen in town and Sade couldn't stay away. She'd go to Mother's room and wouldn't be able to sit still on her chair. You could see she was bursting with it. When she couldn't stand it any more, she'd say, "Now this isn't gossip, Mrs. Morley, just something to make you laugh." Then she'd start in and go as far as she dared. When Mother started to look severe, she'd say, "I've got more to tell you yet, but I guess I better stop now."

❧

Fanny could tell things too, but more decorously. She's very religious. I feel badly she has to be here Sundays and can't go to church. She says she doesn't mind, that she can hear the chimes across the street. She says to me, "Miss Alexandria. Put on your earphones. They're playing hymns." That's when I'm glad I'm deaf. But I don't tell her. She sings along with those bells. I can see her lips move and tell by the saintly look on her face.

❧

From time to time I'd have Bert drive me to Harrisburg. Once Sade asked if she could go along. When Fanny heard, she asked if she could go too. She had several things she wanted to buy. On the way up Sade began to laugh. "Here you are, Miss Alexandria, out for a ride with your chauffeur, your maid and your washerwoman." I looked from one to the other. "Well," I said, "could I find three more faithful and devoted friends?"

On Relatives

NCLE ROB loved horses. He adored them. He had
the same feeling for them Father and I had. He had four
girls and all they were interested in were English novels
and poetry and thin-blooded things like that. "If only they
took to horses like you, Alley," he'd say. He was the only
one I ever let call me that.

❧❦❧

Eulalie always hangs up her stocking. It's an enormous
stocking. Of course, you know, she lives alone and must
fill it herself. She's older than I am but that's what she
does every Christmas.

❧❦❧

Uncle Rob and Aunt Maggie lived till they died in the
big white house overlooking the head of the canal. Aunt

The Aristocrat

Maggie was the daughter of an aristocratic Englishman and fell in love with her father's gamekeeper like in D. H. Lawrence. Only she ran away to America with him. One day her father said to Uncle Rob, "You've been going with my daughter for a year now. When are you going to marry her?" Uncle Rob was thunderstruck. The wedding was arranged. Uncle Rob didn't show up for two hours. He kept everybody waiting. It was all he dared to do to show how he felt about it. You know, English women have a quirk toward men. Their one aim is to get their man fair or foul and their whole life and thought are devoted to it.

❦❦❦

Of Uncle Rob's four girls, only Irene married. She died when her Billy was thirteen years old and Uncle Rob took him in to raise. Aunt Maggie didn't set too rich a table so we had him here for meals when we could. You know how hungry a thirteen-year-old boy can get. They didn't like it and wouldn't let him come any more. So we gave him an allowance to buy something in town when he got hungry. We thought they might stop that, too, but they didn't. We found out afterward when the girls baked a cake, they made Billy pay for a piece of it. I'm sure Uncle Rob never knew but I really don't know what he could have done about it if he had.

❦❦❦

When Uncle Rob was sick, we always tried to send something for him. I'd instruct the maid to insist on taking the basket up to the sick room. If she didn't, Aunt Maggie or one of the girls would pick out something they liked first.

❖❖❖❖

Uncle Caleb and Aunt Liddy lived in that sprawling brick house near Bert Brown's garage in South Unionville. She was from New England, of Scotch descent. We never dared use the word, Scotch, to her. It had to be Scottish. They had only one child, Hallie, but she was as much as four. She and Uncle Rob's girls never got along together or with Blanche and me.

❖❖❖❖

Nothing went on in this town that Grandfather Morley didn't have a hand in. He wrote half the deeds in the county courthouse. He got Col. Morris to come here, also the Hunings and Woodsons and I don't know who all. Half the houses in this town would never have been built if it hadn't been for Grandfather Morley.

❖❖❖❖

They say Cousin Amy was a sweet and charming girl at the time Cousin Harry married her. Then when Rose and

Archie were half grown, she and Ella Beecher went up the aisle of that revival on Chambers Street. They got "happy," threw their hats in the air, told everything they'd done and made fools of themselves generally. People all over town went to see the show. I was heartbroken Mother wouldn't let me go. She said no daughter of hers would ever enter that dreadful place.

❖❖❖❖

Every night Cousin Amy had Archie come in to her bedroom to kiss her good night. She wanted to see if he had been drinking.

❖❖❖❖

Cousin Amy wouldn't allow Rose to buy a thing for herself. Not even after she was twenty-one. Cousin Amy bought her shoes, dresses, underclothing, and hats. Once she let Rose go to the city with me. Mother had some things she wanted me to get for her. Rose asked if she could do it. It was the first time she had ever bought a thing in her life and she got great pleasure out of it. A few months later she was dead from bleeding after a tonsils operation. They didn't know how to take them out then.

❖❖❖❖

One time Cousin Amy offered to bring the salad to our young people's dinner party. Archie said, "Don't put the wine glasses out till she goes. She's just coming to see if you're going to serve alcohol." We always pitied Uncle Harry. We used to invite him along to Harrisburg so he could get away from her. When Bert started the car, Uncle Harry would clap his hands. "Next stop, the Senate!" he'd call out. He meant the old Senate bar on Market Street.

❖❖❖

After Richard and Archie got out of prep school, their fathers put them up in business, gave them the Company store to run. Uncle Asa didn't believe in college. When his father was at the colliery, Richard would ride his pony up the front steps and into the store. You know those steps are almost as many as at the Capitol. To pass the time they'd throw store eggs at a mark on the stable door or play poker with crackers for chips. Crackers came in wooden boxes and barrels those days. They always had somebody on watch at the front door. The minute he'd call, "Your father's coming!" cards would be swept from the table, crackers thrown in the barrel and the pony hurried out the back door. The next fall, Richard went to Yale and Archie to Jefferson Medical School in Philadelphia. And to think they're both gone now.

❖❖❖

The Aristocrat

When Richard got entangled with Tess, I told him to get her a diamond ring. "What must I do that for?" he said. I insisted and went along with him to Bailey, Banks and Biddle to pick it out. He told Tess what I did and Tess said, "If anything ever happens to me, Alix, it will be yours." But I never saw it. Later on she made him buy her a diamond wedding ring, and when she died, that's what she left me. I refused it. What would I want with somebody else's wedding ring? I wouldn't have it, would you, child?

❧❧❧

Richard and I were like brother and sister. When he got mad at me, he'd say he hoped I'd get old and decrepit like Mrs. Kitzmiller without a penny to my name and he'd refuse to take me in and I'd have to live here in one room by myself cooking my own meals in the fireplace and picking my coal off the railroad. I used to shriek and howl listening to him.

❧❧❧

The Markle fund that Richard left in his will has helped put more than a hundred Unionville boys and girls through college. Yet the only time Richard ran for school director, he was defeated by a man who worked in the mines.

159

On Friends

$\mathbf{N}$ORMA CALDER came to see me every year until she died. She told me she never knew what she was worth. I said, wasn't it nice to have so much money you didn't have to bother to find out what your income was. Norma wasn't sure. She said, "When I die, a lot of women will smile on Bill and he'll marry the first one."

◆》《◆《《

Ned was in this house as much as at home. I can still see him down on the floor with Father counting his money. Every Tuesday evening he'd bring it in and Richard would take it over and put it in his bank next day. Ned always said if we hadn't got him saving, he wouldn't have a dime. He spent everything he had on sports. He had his own baseball team. Fay wasn't much better. It was Bert Brown who started him saving. He was our chauffeur. He lived in that stone house at the lower end of town and owned the brick garage next door. He called everybody here by their first names, even our guests. We all liked him. He reminded us of Fred Stone. When we stayed somewhere overnight, our host would put him up in the house. He cried the last time we went to his sickbed and held his hand. "Do you remember the darkies at Sweetwater?" he said. "My people can't understand the way I feel about you. They never knew what it was to be in a family like yours." He always told us when to buy our new car. That was how we got Ned saving. He said, "Girls, you got to do something for Ned. He hasn't paid for his last car yet."

❖❖❖❖❖

Father told us that Bert wasn't really a Brown but a Minnich. His mother was a holy terror and had several children that weren't her husband's. He was an itinerant preacher. Bert knew we knew about this. One time he drove us up to the cemetery to see about seeding the Morley lot. Our cousin, Smiley Morley, from Chamber City was there. He said, "I think it's about time. I've been wondering when you were going to do something about it." When Blanche and I got back to the car, Bert said, "Do you know who that was?" Blanche said, "I think he's a pretty impudent cousin!" "His real name is Smiley Bender," Bert told us. "His mother went over the mountain and had something to do with another man so he's no relation to you at all." We didn't say anything but when we got back to the house, we had a good laugh over it. We knew something about Bert but he knew something about us. I can still see him down in Maryland sitting in the kitchen after dinner smoking his briar pipe and listening to black Aunt Phi talking and rocking and smoking her clay one.

⊹《《⊹《《

Blanche's friend, Rachel, used to spend weeks with us every summer. She was the most beautiful woman but impossible as a guest. She demanded the services of a maid and a doctor full time. She would run Ned to the house at all hours. "Tell her there's nothing wrong with her," he'd say when we telephoned him. Blanche would tell her. "I know dear," she'd say, "but I want your doctor to tell me so himself. He is so sweet and reassuring."

⊹《《⊹《

Another impossible guest was a classmate of Blanche's. I won't mention her name. She came to Blanche's funeral and acted so queer I called Ned to see her. "What's the matter with her?" I asked. "She's drunk," he told me. "What would she get drunk for here and how did she get it?" I asked. "If you don't know, I wouldn't," Ned said.

162

My, my, my that was a night of it! At two o'clock I sent them all to bed.

✧⟨✧⟨

I always said I hoped to die when my stocks are up. I want my heirs to love me at my funeral. I've just been counting up and find I'm very poor. I think I'll go out to Old Mary's in Chickentown to live. Only, I don't think I'd like it. I've always been able to do things for my friends. If Myra Reed or Grace Hoskins needed something, I'd say, here's five or six hundred. Take it and buy what you need. Now it's different. I don't have it any more and I've got to give it up. By jingoes, it's the hardest thing I've ever had to do.

⟨✧⟨✧

The Schuylers are a peculiar family. Miss Cornelia was very strong-willed. One time I had the three sisters to dinner and next day Miss Cornelia called alone. She was very punctilious about paying dinner calls. "I want to tell you something," she said. "I do not wish you to invite me to anything you invite my sisters to. Not ever." I looked at her astonished. "I won't comply," I told her. "Sometimes I will. Sometimes I won't." But I never did. When

The Aristocrat

Miss Cornelia invited us to their summer place, we never knew if her sisters would be there or not.

⤙⟪⤚

When I was a girl, the Schuylers lived in a little house without a bathroom. They had a water closet out on the lot. It was very cold in the winter and when a Miss Dickinson from Philadelphia came to visit them, she'd always carry their lighted oil stove down the walk to keep herself warm out there. Mother didn't want us to play with the Schuylers when we were little. After they built the big house, things were different. Then people were told to call Jennie, Jeanette and Nell, Helen. Miss Cornelia was always Cornelia. After she had that business with Earl Weeks of the Weeks Steel people of Lebanon, Mother forbade her the house.

⤙⟡⟫⤚

Aunt Lou said she thought it a shame that the young men who came here always ate up the candy they brought. Once a victrola arrived with Richard's and Harold Thompson's cards. When they came, I told them they must have spent a hundred and fifty dollars and I'd rather had a riding horse. They just laughed. Of course, I knew why they had sent it. They wanted music while they were

164

here. I never let my head be turned by all the gifts they sent. It wasn't for me but for themselves.

><((><(

Harold Thompson would say on my birthday, "Happy birthday. Gosh, I hope I'll never get as old as you." He was only two years younger and he died before he was forty.

><((><(

Ralph Lewis was a very charming and successful man. He used to run with other women. After Edith Hunting had her long affair with him, Mother wouldn't let her come upstairs. He had a fine home and a very nice wife in Chamber City. One time I had cocktails with him at the Country Club. I called Susie. "I want to tell you before somebody else does," I said. It was a joke between us. Susie told me once, "The secret of Ralph's charm is he never knows when he's not wanted."

><((><(

When the Rev. Davis first came to town, he preached bitterly against liquor. Then he was made chaplain to our national guard company. He went to the Border and

Germany. When he came back and called, I asked him if he would have a Scotch highball. "Why, yes, I will, Miss Alexandria," he said. He would sip and enjoy it. He thought it the most perfect drink ever invented.

On Modern Times

CAN'T READ some of the new novels. When I was a girl, there was a Buel boy down the street who ate worms and manure. He looked like any other child and seemed smarter than most but that's what he went in for. He made a kind of side show out of it. A good many children went to see him and when they saw the notoriety he got, some others tried it. A psychologist today could probably tell you why the Buel boy did it. Perhaps he didn't get attention at home or enough to eat or the right vitamins. The others just wanted to get in on the act. Blanche and I weren't finicky. We ate snails in France and octopus in Greece. But we never acquired a taste for manure. It's one of the few things ever made me wonder if there might be something in this reincarnation business. I can imagine what that boy might have been beforehand. This was nearly eighty years ago and what happened to him since I never heard.

The Aristocrat

I read somewhere that this new kind of novel is supposed to be moralistic. I guess nobody wants to admit he's in the dirt business. Even the commercial people like to call their product sand or soil or crushed trap rock or something respectable. We girls kicked over the traces pretty far in our day and against a great deal more opposition than now, but we never fooled ourselves that we were moralistic or were liberating the world. We did it for devilment, to be one step ahead of the crowd. A year or so ago the superintendent of the Sunday School that Fanny went to was arrested for selling worthless stocks to his own poor church people. His preacher went to see him in the penitentiary. The convict sat in his cell and told him they weren't running the church right and how from A to Z they ought to do it. It greatly amused me when Fanny told me, Barabbas telling St. Peter how to get to heaven.

❖❖❖

The sanitation engineer has other names for the filth down on the dump, fancy scientific names. I suppose his stock in trade seems more respectable to him that way. But it didn't make it smell any sweeter to me.

❖❖❖

When someone didn't pay a dinner call, Mother wiped the name off her list and never invited that person again.

It's good she isn't alive today. I know nice young people graduated from high school and college who won't or can't write a letter of thanks for a thirty-five-dollar wedding gift. They buy a fifteen-cent printed thank-you card at the store. If they're very proper, they write in some line like, "It was just what we wanted." I understand Ed Rabey's store sells all kinds of printed cards, birthday cards, anniversary cards, get well cards, anything to save you from writing a note. It's a sign of our uncivilized times. These modern young people know how to use a hundred gadgets I can do without, but they've dropped behind the Pennsylvania Dutch farmer when I was a girl. He couldn't say thanks for a favor, either. He didn't know how. But a few mornings later you'd wake up and find a chicken or bushel of potatoes on your back doorstep.

❖❐❖❐

Beauty's a Victorian word. It's gone out of style now with the Victorians. People still use it today but for strange reasons. They call the place where you get a permanent a beauty shop. This town used to know beauty. Now the trees and charm are gone. Even the farmer used to live by a kind of beauty. His shocked wheat and corn fields straightened out something in your mind and his. Now his fields are simply ravaged. His cows used to stand knee deep in pasture. Now more and more of them stand knee deep in manure in his dairy lot. It smells to high heaven when you go by. I wonder about the milk, that the health inspectors let people drink it. I've sworn off. I won't touch a drop.

❖❖❖

The powers that be are trying to turn us into sheep. We must tell the government what we earn and how much we save. We must stop when the traffic signal says stop and go when it says go. We must break off interesting radio or television programs until the commercials are rammed down our throats. It's one way of making people meek and submissive for what's coming. But it doesn't me. I say, to the devil with you, and turn off my set.

❖❖❖

When I was young, I thought democracy a wonderful thing. Now I see a monarchy is better. You can love and respect a king but you have to have a good one. It's a risk you take but not any more than when you vote for a politician. That nice, polite Italian, Dagostino, who brings me vegetables, knows that some people are better than others. Our country hasn't found it out yet. Everybody thinks himself a fit architect for his own house. Look at some of the new ones. They tell me they cost a lot of money and only a few have any lines. Thirty years from now, if they don't fall down, most of them will look like sheds or Grant's tomb. But I don't have to live in them. That's their lookout. What bothers me is their music. Any small-time orchestra leader thinks he knows more than the composer. So he changes the music to suit himself. Toscanini could have done it and wouldn't. But the democracy boys think they can. It's the modern dispensation.

◈❮◈❮◈

I guess you're too young to remember how the old stone church used to look inside. People who knew called it the most perfect specimen of Colonial architecture around here. Then they got a young minister cracked on democracy. He tore it apart and rebuilt it to suit his own ideas. It made me raving mad. I told him he was a vandal and a Hitler burning the books. He didn't like it. He's the same one I read the law off to for never opening the door of the car for his wife.

◈❮◈❮◈

These days you're not supposed to get mad. They say it's murder on your blood vessels. I don't only get mad but I kick the swinging door as I go through. It's such a handy place to take it out on.

171

On Herself
and Other Things

DON'T KNOW what it costs to join the Country Club. We never had to join. We founded it and decided who we wanted in and who we wanted kept out. Even so some of those people got in.

◆《◆《◆

I was only eighteen when I had to wear glasses. Mother and Father wouldn't believe it. They thought you put on glasses only when you got old. I went to Alexander Graham Bell's eye doctor in Washington, a German. He said, "You say you do embroidery. How do you see to do it?" I could see better at once with his glasses. Mother said when I got home, "Take off those glasses. No young lady should disfigure her face like that till she's married."

◆《◆《◆

The Aristocrat

I invested in another hearing aid today. I didn't need any but it's supposed to be brand-new and Mr. Mayberry is such a gentleman. His manners were the only thing that made me try one on in the first place. "Can you hear me now?" he asked the first time I put one on. I was delighted. I said, "Say something more." "How old are you?" he asked. I took his hearing aid off and told him no gentleman would say that to a lady. Then I saw he was laughing. He did it only to bait me and we've been the best of friends ever since.

❖❙❐❖❐❐

We always had a good time in this house. One Sunday Aunt Lou came in while we were playing Going to Jerusalem in the dining room. I can still see her standing horrified in the doorway. She went straight up to Mother. "Lolly, do you know what's going on in this Christian house on the Sabbath day?" "Is this your house or mine?" Mother asked. "Yours, Lolly." "Then you needn't worry, I gave them permission." I think our best game was playing fireman with seltzer bottles. Mother would hear us howl and scream and say, "I'm glad you had a good time, girls. Just don't do anything to make our maids leave us." Father never heard us. All he'd say was "Do you have enough money for your party, girls?"

❖❙❐❖❐❐

The Aristocrat

I went to Mrs. Somers' school in Washington. It was called Mt. Vernon Seminary then. Alexander Graham Bell's daughters were my schoolmates. Mrs. Somers had twelve at-homes during the year. Foreign ambassadors would come. Four girls would stand in the receiving line. The butler would bring the guests in and announce them. Then one of the girls would take them to the two large living rooms where the tea tables were. If you spoke one word about the weather, you were never asked in the receiving line again.

❖❙❖❙❖

I've had insomnia all my life. Once at school there was a tap on my door and Mrs. Somers stepped in. It was after midnight. "Alexandria, what are you doing?" she said. "I'm lying on the floor on my stomach reading with an umbrella over me to shut out the light and now you've seen me," I told her. "Don't you know the rules?" she asked. "Yes, of course, I do, but I can't lie in bed and twiddle my thumbs all night. It makes me too nervous." "I know. It does me, too," Mrs. Somers said. "That's why I'm walking the halls," and she went out and closed the door.

❖❙❖❙❖

The Aristocrat

They were splendid cultured people from the town of the Halls murder case.

❖❖❖❖

My nice little asparagus woman always comes in and hunts me up. But she wonders if she should. "My!" she said. "If I had somebody walk in on me like this in my own house, it would scare the daylights out of me."

❖❖❖❖

I don't keep money in the house. When I need five dollars for this or ten for that, I borrow from Fanny. She's my banker.

❖❖❖❖

It's always been the turkey carver's privilege in this house to cut out the two small bits of tenderloin on the bird's back for himself.

❖❖❖❖

I was as near to Brahms as I am to you. Klineworth, too. You've surely heard of him. He arranged Chopin's music. His name was always on it. He was Hope's friend.

1 7 5

He knew I don't know how many languages. Hope spoke seven.

❖❖❖❖

They say the best comes after forty. I've been looking for it.

❖❖❖❖

And now they want me to put a lavatory in downstairs. Dr. Howell says I daren't run the stairs any more. Perhaps I should. What I can't stand is the idea of one lavatory already in the basement and four or five bathrooms upstairs and only one person living in the house besides you.

❖❖❖❖

I hear that townspeople say I'm common. They don't use the word like we do. They mean I don't care what old clothes I go around in and like Mother, I speak to everybody.

❖❖❖❖

Two Mormon missionaries came to see me last year. They were young and very nice. I let them stay an hour and a half. They might have converted me if they hadn't told me that Mormons weren't allowed to drink, smoke or play poker. They wanted to pray for me. I said all right. I couldn't kneel but since I wasn't sick we could stand. I swear my asthma was better after they said whatever they said.

❧⟐❧

Hope's young man from Baltimore told me I was quite interesting for a country woman. I could have slapped his face. But I smiled and was amused.

❧⟐❧

Mr. January is upset about his children. It's cost him thousands to send his oldest to college and now she wants to go to graduate school. "And remember I have four more," he said. "You brought them into the world," I told him, "and you'll have to educate them, every one."

❧⟐❧

I hope nothing happens to me while Dr. Howell is away. He stands between me and all that (waving her arms toward the hospital and cemetery).

❧⟐❧

The Aristocrat

My, my, my, Agnes Richardson is such a lady. She wouldn't do anything except as we do it.

❖❐❖❐

Princess Vershaliv said to me, "Yes, I knew Alfred Noyes on the Isle of Wight. In fact I lived with him for three years. I suppose that isn't exactly a nice thing to say." "No," I told her. "It's a perfectly terrible thing to say. But how interesting."

Cast of Characters
Living and Dead

MISS ALEXANDRIA F. MORLEY
CAPTAIN ARCHIBALD MORLEY, her father
MRS. OLIVIA (LOLLY) FORTUNE MORLEY, her mother
MISS BLANCHE F. MORLEY (MRS. ROSECOMMON),
  Miss Alexandria's sister
MISS HOPE F. MORLEY, the eldest sister
HOPE CONNOR, granddaughter of Hope Morley, married to a
  Lutheran minister

ROBERT NEFF MORLEY, an uncle
AUNT MAGGIE MORLEY, his wife
IRENE, OLGA, LILIAN, HORTENSE MORLEY, daughters
BILLY COUTTS, Irene's son

CALEB MORLEY, an uncle
LYDIA MORLEY, his wife
MISS HALLIE MORLEY (MRS. HOMER JONES), a daughter

MRS. FREDERICA LOUISA MORLEY SCARLETT (AUNT LOU),
  sister of Alexandria's father
THE REV. TIMOTHY SCARLETT, her husband

The Aristocrat

JIM MORLEY, a brother of Captain Morley

MOLLY CRUMP MORLEY, Jim's wife

YOUNG TOMMY GAULT, their great-grandson who tells the narrative

MARTIN GAULT, his father

MISS EULALIE (MRS. JACK FERGUSON), Miss Alexandria's cousin

UNCLE SAM FORTUNE, Miss Eulalie's father

AUNT SUDY (MRS. SUSAN FORTUNE), his wife

MRS. EULALIE SMITH, Miss Eulalie's namesake, of no relation

ASA MARKLE, Miss Alexandria's uncle

AUNT RUBY FORTUNE MARKLE, his wife

LUCY MARKLE, their daughter

RICHARD MARKLE, their son

TESS GORMAN MARKLE, Richard's wife and widow

"COUSIN" HARRY MARKLE, Asa's brother

"COUSIN" AMY MARKLE, his wife

"COUSIN" ARCHIE, their son

"COUSIN" ROSE, their daughter

FANNY, POLLY, OLD MARY, SADE, CARRIE, ROXIE, maids

DR. CLAY HOWELL, Miss Alexandria's present physician

DR. EDWARD (NED) TEMPLE, her former doctor and friend

MRS. FAY TEMPLE, his wife

THE REV. DANNER, Lutheran minister and neighbor

MR. JANUARY, Miss Alexandria's lawyer

The Aristocrat

BENNY STETLER, Unionville undertaker
MISS CORNELIA SCHUYLER, a neighbor
MISS JENNIE (JEANETTE) SCHUYLER, a sister
MISS NELL (HELEN) SCHUYLER, a sister
MISS ELEANOR FITZGIBBON, a cousin and heir of the Schuylers
MR. CARPENTER, the Schuyler attorney
EDWARD HASSLER, Sunday School superintendent

A NOTE ABOUT THE AUTHOR

CONRAD RICHTER was born in Pennsylvania, the son, grandson, nephew, and great-nephew of clergymen. He was intended for the ministry, but at thirteen he declined a scholarship and left preparatory school for high school, from which he graduated at fifteen. After graduation he went to work. His family on his mother's side was identified with the early American scene, and from boyhood on he was saturated with tales and the color of Eastern pioneer days. In 1928 he and his small family moved to New Mexico, where his heart and mind were soon captured by the Southwest. From this time on he devoted himself to fiction. *The Sea of Grass* and *The Trees* were awarded the gold medal of the Societies of Libraries of New York University in 1942. *The Town* received the Pulitzer Prize in 1951, and *The Waters of Kronos* won the 1960 National Book Award for fiction. His other novels include *The Fields* (1946), *The Light in the Forest* (1953), *The Lady* (1957), and *A Country of Strangers* (1966).

A NOTE ON THE TYPE

THE TEXT of this book was set on the Linotype in
Janson, a recutting made direct from type cast from
matrices long thought to have been made by the
Dutchman Anton Janson, who was a practicing type
founder in Leipzig during the years 1668–87. However, it has been conclusively demonstrated that these
types are actually the work of Nicholas Kis (1650–
1702), a Hungarian, who most probably learned his
trade from the master Dutch type founder Dirk
Voskens. The type is an excellent example of the
influential and sturdy Dutch types that prevailed in
England up to the time William Caslon developed
his own incomparable designs from these Dutch faces.

Composed, printed, and bound by
The Book Press, Incorporated, Brattleboro, Vt.
Binding based on original design
by W. A. Dwiggins

DATE DUE

APR 1 1 2023	
	PRINTED IN U.S.A.